WILD HEART

TYSON WILD BOOK TWENTY FOUR

TRIPP ELLIS

WELCOME

Want more books like this?

You'll probably never hear about my new releases unless you join my newsletter.

SIGN UP HERE

nd that was the last time you saw him?" I asked.

Brody nodded.

It was two weeks ago when we spoke with Brody Kempner about his missing friend, Emmett Forrester.

Brody was a late-20s IT guy for a local law firm. He maintained their servers, data storage, and handled Internet marketing. It was a good job. I don't think he had to work too hard.

He lived in the same apartment complex as Emmett, and the two had been childhood friends. As Brody explained, they had met in 2nd grade and maintained their friendship all through high school and college. They were roommates at the University of Texas.

Brody was an average-looking guy. 5'10", brown hair, brown eyes, and an oval-shaped face. He was relatively trim but wasn't exactly putting the hours in at the gym. The only exercise he got was lifting a bottle of beer to his lips. It was starting to show around his waistline.

He had a comfortable life, making good money with a nice apartment a few blocks from the beach. A quick look around his place told me that he had all the toys a young man could want—65" flatscreen TV, surround sound stereo system, leather furniture, and a signature model guitar in the corner with a small practice amp. From the balcony of the apartment, you could see the teal ocean in the distance.

Brody sat on the couch in the living room. JD and I sat across from him.

"Yeah," Brody continued. "We were at *Turtles* having a few beers."

"And when was that?" I asked.

"That was Thursday night, week before last."

"So you're at the bar, having a few beers. Then what?"

"I had to work in the morning, so we shut it down about midnight. Plus, my girlfriend was blowing up my phone. She gets a little nervous when I'm out past midnight with my friends. You know how it is."

"What's your girlfriend's name?"

"Allison Dobbs."

"That's the last time you saw Emmett, but you waited another week and a half to make a missing persons' report?" There was a slightly accusatory tone in my voice.

"I didn't think anything was wrong. Emmett was leaving Friday to go to Aspen on a ski trip with a bunch of guys we went to college with." A slight frown tugged his face. "I was supposed to go with them, but I had to bail at the last minute. Allison's father took ill and was in the hospital. If I ever wanted to get laid again, I'd have to cancel my trip and offer moral support."

"How is her father doing?" I asked.

"Not great. He just had heart valve surgery, then he got an infection and went septic. So, he was in for several days. They didn't think he was gonna make it, but he pulled through."

"It's a good thing you didn't go skiing," JD said.

Brody shrugged. "I guess."

"What about your college buddies in Aspen? Have they heard anything from Emmett?"

Brody shook his head. "No. I just talked to Jason. He hasn't heard anything."

"Didn't your friends get worried when Emmett didn't show up in Aspen?"

"They thought when I canceled my trip that Emmett wasn't going either. So, when he didn't show up in Aspen, they didn't think anything about it. It was supposed to be this big party week. Once a year, we all try to get together and go skiing. We booze all night, ski all day, and chase snow bunnies. The plan was to leave Friday, ski the weekend, the entire week, and the next weekend, then come back late Sunday night." Brody sighed, and his shoulders slumped.

"When did you start getting concerned?" I asked.

"I didn't expect to hear from Emmett until Monday. I knew he would call and tell me what I missed and how awesome it was. I was curious, but I was also dreading that call. That's why I didn't bother to reach out to those guys during the trip. I figured I'd hear all about it later. I didn't want to know what I was missing. And they would just razz me about my girlfriend not letting me go."

"You called the department yesterday," I said.

"Yeah. I didn't hear from Emmett Monday. Didn't hear from him Tuesday. That's when I called Jason, and he said Emmett never showed up."

"And where is Jason?"

"He lives in Vegas."

"Does Emmett have family in town?" I asked.

Brody shook his head again. "No. His parents live in Austin."

"Have you spoken with them?"

"I have. They haven't heard from Emmett since before he was supposed to leave."

"Was he close with his parents?"

"I guess. Sort of. His mom and dad are divorced, and they've each got their own thing going on. Emmett talked to them once every couple of weeks, so it wasn't unusual for him to go radio silent for a few weeks."

"How did you guys end up in Coconut Key?"

"We used to come down here for spring break all the time. It just seemed awesome. After graduation, we were like *fuck it, let's move here. Let's party all the time. It will be spring break all year round.* We've been here ever since."

"You said Emmett lives in this apartment complex."

"Yeah, he's just down the hall. I've got keys to his apartment and his car. His car is in the parking garage. And his apartment looks undisturbed. Hell, his suitcase is still half packed." He paused, thinking. "You guys can check flight records, right? I don't think he ever left town."

"You've got the keys to his apartment?"

"Yeah, do you want me to show you the place?"

2

W e found something odd.

Emmett's one-bedroom apartment looked exactly like Brody's but with different furniture and different art on the walls. The cookie-cutter floor plans made all the units in the *Calliste Apartments* look the same.

We searched the apartment, and there was no sign of a struggle. The bed was made, and Emmett's suitcase sat atop the comforter. The lid was open, and the roller-case was half full with folded clothes, underwear, socks, etc. The toiletries were still in the bathroom.

Odd.

"What time was Emmett's flight out on Friday?" I asked.

"8:55 AM," Brody said.

The bed didn't look like it had been slept in. It was like Emmett had vanished into thin air.

"Did Emmett have any enemies?"

Brody shook his head. "Not that I know of."

"What about a girlfriend?"

"He broke up with Lauren about four months ago. Ever since then, he's been on a rampage, chasing it." Brody grinned mischievously.

"I guess that creates a little trouble for you, being his wing-man," JD said.

Brody gave an enthusiastic nod. "You have no idea. I mean, I am the guy who's always gotta spoil the party at the end of the night. I can't go to the after-hours clubs with him and two hotties." He frowned.

"The sacrifices we make for love," JD said.

We left Emmett's apartment, and Brody locked it up afterward.

"You said his car is still here?" I asked.

Brody nodded. "Yeah. It's in the parking garage below the building. I don't think it's moved since he went missing."

"Can we take a look?" I asked.

Brody nodded and led us down the hallway to the elevator bank. He pressed the call button. A moment later, the bell rang, and the doors slid open. We plunged down to the parking garage that was located beneath the structure. Large, cylindrical concrete pylons supported the building, each labeled with a section number. Fluorescent overheads illuminated the place at night. All the spaces were numbered and assigned.

We followed Brody across the lot to a Lexus coupe. It was midnight blue with a beige interior—sleek, graceful lines, with shiny rims and glossy tires.

There was a strong breeze gusting through the parking garage. The architecture created a natural tunnel that funneled wind through the structure. The gusts blew JD's long, blond hair like he was in a music video.

I looked around the car and peered in through the window. The car was clean, and there was nothing unusual about it.

There was a dumpster in the alley behind the garage. Now and then, when the wind would die down, I'd get a whiff of something rank. I jogged out of the garage and peered in through the sliding side hatch of the battered green dumpster. The heinous smell from years of oozing trash slapped my face and crinkled my nose.

The inside of the dumpster was coated with an indescribable slime that had fused with the metal. No amount of scrubbing could ever get this thing clean. It smelled like rotten eggs, fish, urine, and decaying meat. The trash bin had recently been emptied, and there were only a few bags inside.

No trace of Emmett.

I jogged back to the parking garage and re-joined JD and Brody. "Since the car is in the parking garage, I'm guessing Emmett made it home from *Turtles* on Thursday night. Something must have happened between the garage and his apartment." My eyes scanned the area, looking for security cameras. "Is the management office on the premises?"

Brody nodded and took us to the second floor.

Patti managed the building. She smiled as we entered the office, but that faded when we flashed our badges and were no longer prospective tenants.

"What can I do for you?" she asked.

Patti sat behind a desk with a computer terminal and a picture of her daughter in a frame beside the monitor. She was late 50s with short blonde hair and too much blue eyeliner. The leather office chair struggled to contain her pear-shaped body.

"I'd like to see the security camera footage for the parking garage," I said.

"Sorry, don't have any."

"What do you mean? I saw cameras."

"Those are dummy cameras. They've been amazingly effective. We don't have as many smash and grabs as we used to."

I grimaced.

"What's the problem?" she asked.

I told her the situation.

She gasped. "That's terrible." Then, without much of a pause, "I guess Emmett's going to miss next month's rent."

Brody's eyes narrowed at her, but he bit his tongue.

I think Patti picked up on the tension. "I do hope he's okay."

"Can you speak with the tenants? Maybe somebody saw something."

"And you say this was Thursday before last?"

"Yes, ma'am."

"I can send an email out to all the residents."

"That would be wonderful. Thank you."

I gave Patti and Brody a card.

We left the office and stepped into the hallway.

"Call me if you can think of anything else," I said to Brody.

"What happens now?"

"We'll ask around and follow leads. We'll notify the FBI. You may be hearing from them."

Brody nodded. Then his face tightened. "You don't think Emmett's dead, do you?"

"It's too soon to speculate," I said, not wanting to alarm him.

But Brody was already alarmed. "This is bad, right? I mean, adults don't just disappear like that."

"People go missing all the time," I said, "but they usually turn up in a few days." I paused. "I'm not gonna lie. This is concerning."

Brody frowned.

"We'll talk to his employer, and I'll keep you updated if we learn anything new. By the way, do you have a picture of Emmett handy?"

"Yeah, I've got a few on my phone. Hang on." He pulled out the device and scrolled through the camera roll. He pulled up a picture of the two in a bar, holding up two longnecks to the camera. "I'll text it to you."

A moment later, the image buzzed my phone. I pulled it up, zoomed in on Emmett's face and cropped the image, cutting Brody out. It wasn't the best photo in the world, but it would do for now.

We thanked Brody again, then took the elevator down to the lobby. We stepped outside and crossed the visitors' parking lot to Jack's convertible Porsche. We climbed in, and JD twisted the ignition. He dropped the sports car into gear and pulled out of the lot.

I called Denise as we drove with the top down, the wind swirling about. The Florida sun beamed down, and classic rock pumped from the speakers.

"Hey, can you double-check something for me? I don't think our missing person made it to the airport, but check the flight's manifest just in case." I gave her the airline and the flight number Brody had given me.

"I'm on it," Denise said.

We headed across town to an orthopedic clinic where Emmett worked. The place was a one-stop shop for all your bone and joint needs. There were seven different physicians in the practice, each specializing in a different area—hips, knees, hands, feet, spine, neck, shoulders.

The facility was connected to a surgical center and a rehab facility. One of the biggest risks with joint replacement is infection. A surgery center that is not connected to a major hospital typically has a lower incidence of infection due to the lack of sick patients coming and going. This group of doctors had the process down. They churned through patients like an assembly line. The high volume made the practice one of the most experienced on the island.

There were large pictures of people of all ages participating in sports—jogging, tennis, cycling, soccer, golf. The images all had the name of the clinic in the corner, and the slogan was emblazoned in a large font, "We get you back in action!"

A cute brunette behind the reception desk greeted us with a cheery smile when we flashed our badges. "I'd like to speak to someone about Emmett Forrester."

3

"I gotta be honest with you," Steve Jackson said. "This is distressing. I can't think of a nicer, more likable guy than Emmett Forrester. He's a real asset around the clinic. And I think I can speak for the entire staff when I say he is not only liked but respected."

Steve was the owner. He wore a charcoal suit, white dress shirt, and a red tie. His teeth were pearly white, and he had a square jaw and perfectly coiffed hair.

He led us down a hallway to his office. He motioned for us to step inside and offered us a seat. Everything about the clinic was sleek and modern, and his office was no different. He had a frosted glass desk with a brand-new iMac. There was a flatscreen display and wireless speakers. A financial news channel played on the TV with the volume muted. Floor-to-ceiling windows offered a view of the hedges and the parking lot. It was the only thing that wasn't impressive about the clinic.

Steve pulled the door shut behind us and took a seat at his desk. "Can I get you anything to drink? Bottled water?"

We both declined his offer.

"Did Emmett have any conflicts with any of his coworkers?" I asked.

"As I said, he really has helped take the clinic to the next level, and I've never heard any of the physicians or staff speak ill of him." He sighed and shook his head. "He informed us of his vacation plans, but when he didn't show up for work on Monday, it was unusual. I called his phone several times and left messages—no reply. I thought maybe there was some travel delay. Understandable. I called Tuesday—nothing. I was starting to get worried, and I can't say that I'm shocked to see you boys here. I just had this gut instinct that something was wrong. Emmett is not one to leave you hanging. I don't think he's ever taken a sick day since he's been here."

"How long has he been working for you?"

"Oh, I'd say about three years now."

"What was Emmett's role here?"

"Operations Manager. Staffing, logistics, advertising—that kind of thing. He really kept this place rolling. Emmett had a knack for people. He could look at a candidate right away and tell if they would be a good fit for this environment. That was one of his main assets."

"So, he was in charge of hiring and firing?"

Steve nodded. "That's correct."

"Has anyone been recently terminated?"

Steve thought for a moment. "We haven't had to let anybody go in over a year."

"And who was that?"

"Stacy Taft."

"Why was she terminated?"

"I'd have to check the records, but poor performance as I recall. All employees have quarterly performance evaluations. We measure certain empirical factors as well as intangibles. I like to think we provide a wonderful work environment here. All you need to do is show up on time, do your job, maintain a positive attitude, and treat patients with dignity and respect."

"I take it Stacy wasn't doing that?"

"Again, I would have to check the files, but as I recall, she was quite often late, would miss work without calling, and generally had an unpleasant demeanor. We got a lot of patient complaints. In the end, she wasn't a fit. We're a high-performance organization."

"I'll need her contact information," I said.

"Certainly. But she was let go a year ago. Do you really think she'd still be harboring a grudge?"

"We like to keep all possibilities open," I said.

Steve's brow knitted together, and he stared at me curiously. "You're treating this like Emmett is deceased. Is there something you're not telling me?"

"We have no reason to believe that is the case," I said. "But..."

Steve frowned.

He pulled up Stacy's record on his computer and printed a copy of her employment file. He snatched the pages from the printer and handed them across the desk to me. "That's the last known information I have for her. I'm not sure how accurate it is, but I'm sure you two deputies can find her."

I nodded.

We thanked him for his time, and Steve escorted us from his office. He ushered us back to the main lobby. "Please don't hesitate to contact me if you have further questions."

We pushed through the glass doors and stepped into the parking lot.

"What do you think?" JD asked.

"I think we need to go to *Turtles* and ask around."

We hopped into JD's Porsche, and he cranked up the engine. He dropped it into gear and launched out of the parking lot. We zipped across the island to Oyster Avenue.

Denise called along the way. "I talked to the airline. Emmett never boarded flight UW 2379."

"Not surprising. See if the phone company will hand over his records. If not, talk to Daniels about getting a subpoena."

"Don't you have connections for that?" she asked in a slightly snarky tone.

"I do. And that's my next call, but we may need legitimate evidence at some point."

"Is there anything else?"

"That's all for now. I'm sure I'll think of something else."

"I'm sure you will."

I ended the call, then dialed Isabella. She was my handler at *Cobra Company*. The clandestine agency could get their hands on just about any piece of data floating around in the aether. Acquiring phone records would be easy. *Cobra Company's* methods weren't always legal but were effective.

I asked Isabella if she could track Emmett's phone and give me a current location. I gave her the cell number and heard her fingers clack against a keyboard. Within a few moments, Isabella said, "That phone is not on the grid."

"When was the last time it pinged a cell tower?"

"Thursday before last at 1:32 AM."

"Where?"

"2222 Buena Vista Drive."

That was the address to Emmett's apartment building.

"Nothing after that?"

"Nothing," she said.

I thanked her for the information and ended the call.

Jack weaved through town and pulled to the curb on Oyster Avenue, not far from *Turtles*. Tourists strolled the avenue, staggering from bar to bar. At this time of day, the avenue wasn't very crowded, but there was always a festive atmosphere on the island. It was never too early for a cocktail.

The strip was lined with bars and restaurants, and the smell of food filled the air. At night, the avenue would light up with a kaleidoscope of colors, and live music would spill into the streets. There was always a good time, or hangover, to be found on Oyster Avenue.

Turtles was one of many tropical-themed beach bars. The tabletops were painted to look like turtle shells, and murals of sea turtles were painted on the walls. The place smelled like beer and strawberry daiquiris. There was a good crowd in the daytime, but nothing compared to what happened there at night. The place would pack up with sweaty bodies squeezing past one another.

We made our way to the main bar, and JD flashed his shiny gold badge. I showed the bartender Emmett's picture on my phone. "Do you recognize this guy?"

"Yeah, he looks familiar," the bartender said. "He's in here pretty regularly."

"Do you remember seeing him Thursday before last?" I asked.

He thought about it for a moment. "I can't really say. One day blends into the next around here, you know what I mean?"

A cute waitress sauntered up to the bar. She hovered close and looked at the image on my phone. "Yeah, I remember seeing that guy. But I can't tell you exactly when."

"I'll print out some *missing* fliers," I said. "You mind if I come back and post them?"

"Sure, go ahead," the bartender said.

"If you can remember anything, give me a call." I handed him a card.

We left the bar and strolled the sidewalk back to the car.

Over the next few days, I spoke with Emmett's parents and pulled his credit card records. There had been no activity since his disappearance. The last charge on his credit card was at *Turtles* after midnight. He'd closed out his tab and headed home.

The case went cold, and there was no movement over the next two weeks. I was beginning to think this would slip away into the unsolved abyss.

4

———

"Got any big plans for Valentine's Day?" Teagan asked. The slight arch in her eyebrow told me this was more than just mere curiosity.

Teagan had decorated *Diver Down* with hearts and cut-outs of Cupid ready to sling arrows at unsuspecting lovers.

"I haven't given it much thought, actually," I said.

"Well, I've had no shortage of offers since you guys released the music video. It's been insane."

It wasn't surprising. The teal-eyed beauty was gorgeous with a perfect, petite little figure. She wore a teeny bikini top that hugged her all-natural endowments. She had a flat stomach and wore cut-off jean shorts that barely covered her round cheeks. She'd been featured in the music video for *All I Need,* which had catapulted JD's band to Internet stardom. *Wild Fury* needed a follow-up to avoid *one-hit wonder* status, and I had no doubt they had more hits in them.

"My social media has totally blown up, and the number of dick pics I get every day is staggering," Teagan continued. "Why do guys feel the need to do that? It's totally not a turn on."

"Girls send me topless photos of themselves all the time," JD said with a grin.

"Yeah, but that's different," Teagan said. "Guys like that kind of thing. You're visual creatures. I can guarantee you that no girl ever got a random dick pic and said, *oh yeah, I gotta have that.*"

We chuckled.

She sighed. "I don't know, it's kind of freaking me out. Somehow, these people have figured out my address and my cell phone number." She reached under the counter and produced a sub-compact 9mm Bösch-Haüer. "So I got this."

JD and I both raised our eyebrows.

"Don't worry, it's not loaded," Teagan assured, setting it atop the bar.

"Do you mind?" I asked before picking it up.

She nodded.

I press-checked the weapon, making sure there wasn't a round in the chamber. My thumb pressed the mag release button, and the magazine dropped into my palm.

It was empty.

The pistol felt good in my hand. It was well-balanced.

"Did I do good?" Teagan asked.

"Yes, you did. I'm impressed."

"I had to fill out one of those forms and pass a background check. Does that mean I'm in some type of database now?"

"Technically, no. But those forms are kept on file with the firearms dealer, so that weapon would be traceable back to you in the event of a crime. And the ATF has been known to photograph the records when they do inspections."

Teagan gave me a sassy look. "I can assure you, I'm not committing any crimes with that weapon. This is for emergency self-defense purposes only. I have no intention of ever using it outside the range." She paused, then made an adorable face. "So, maybe that can be my Valentine's Day present? You can take me to the gun range. I've already taken a basic gun safety course, but I want some expert guidance."

"Where do I sign up?" JD asked.

She smiled. "I'm off tomorrow. Does that work for you guys?"

"I believe we can make that work," I said

Teagan bounced up and down with excitement. "Yay!"

She had a nice bounce. Things jiggled in magical ways, and I think Cupid fired a few arrows.

"You might want to put that away before you scare the customers," I said, nodding to the pistol.

Teagan grabbed the weapon and put it back beneath the bar.

"Do not let that out of your sight. You don't want that thing walking off."

"I know," she said. "I'll take good care of it."

My phone buzzed in my pocket. I pulled it out and looked at the caller ID. It was Sheriff Daniels. I swiped the screen and held the phone to my ear.

"Tell me you've got a lead on Emmett Forrester," I said.

The sheriff's gruff voice filtered through the speaker, "Nope. But I've got something else you boys might be interested in."

I cringed.

"Get down to the station ASAP," Daniels continued. "The Coast Guard found a boat with two dead bodies on it."

"We'll be right there." I ended the call and filled JD in on the situation.

I said goodbye to Teagan, and we pushed out of the bar, darted across the parking lot, and hopped into the Porsche.

Sheriff Daniels had a patrol boat ready by the time we arrived at the station. We hustled down the dock and boarded the aluminum Defender class patrol boat. Brenda, the medical examiner, joined us along with a forensics team.

We cast off, and Sheriff Daniels idled out of the marina. He throttled up, bringing the boat on plane, and the hull carved through the swells, spraying salty mists. The engines rumbled, spitting a frothy trail as we headed across the turquoise water toward *Eel Reef*.

5

A 131-foot, tri-deck *SunTrekker* yacht was moored to a buoy near *Eel Reef*. Crafted with sleek lines and made from the finest materials, the *SunTrekker* was the pinnacle of luxury. With a 27' beam, a draft of 9'6", and accommodations for 12, the oasis on the water was the ideal cruiser for those chasing an endless summer. It could accommodate a crew of 8 and had a range of 1,600 nautical miles.

A shiny chrome name board read *Dirty Talk* across the garage.

A Coast Guard patrol boat hovered nearby, and two petty officers waited on the aft deck of the *Dirty Talk*.

We pulled to the swim platform, tied off, and boarded the vessel. Sheriff Daniels, Brenda, and the forensics team followed.

A petty officer greeted us. We made introductions, then he said, "I'll show you to it."

We crossed the aft deck that had an alfresco dining area. The petty officer pulled open the sliding glass door to the salon and led us forward across the lounge, past the formal dining area.

The fit and finish of the boat were second to none. The furniture was modern and elegant. There was a minibar in the lounge and a day head to port. Large windows allowed copious amounts of light to bathe the compartment. The boat had clean, graceful lines. The design had been well thought out.

We followed the petty officer through a passageway on the starboard side that led to the master stateroom. We passed a central staircase that spiraled above and below deck. To port was a full galley with a stovetop, ice maker, refrigerator, microwave, dishwasher, a breakfast table and settee.

The petty officer paused just outside the master stateroom and cautioned, "I have to warn you, it's pretty rank."

He took a deep breath, held it, then pushed open the hatch. With a grimace, he stood aside and allowed us to enter.

The pungent smell was like a punch to the nose. Sour and rotten. It instantly twisted my stomach and activated my gag reflex. Breakfast rumbled in my belly in an uncomfortable way. I'd smelled some pretty atrocious things in my day, but this was up there with the worst of them. My face twisted, and so did the expressions of my compatriots—except for Brenda. Brenda was immune to this kind of thing.

Flies buzzed about as we stepped inside. My eyes scanned the horrific scene.

The luxurious stateroom spanned the full beam of the ship. From the ceiling, a flatscreen display folded down. There was a small lounge area with a table and two chairs to starboard. To port, there was a dresser. There were *his* and *hers* closets, and a full beam en suite with *his* and *hers* sinks, tub, and shower stall. Windows opened on the port and starboard sides to allow a seamless blend of interior and exterior spaces.

It would have been paradise but for the crimson blood that speckled the bed sheets and splattered the bulkheads.

The body of a naked man lay on the deck beside the bed.

A naked woman lay atop the queen berth—her arms were outstretched, and her legs spread wide. The body had clearly been positioned after death. In her mouth, the killer had stuffed an oversized silicone sex toy, and her blank eyes stared at the ceiling. They were now milky with haze.

There were two small-caliber bullet wounds to her chest—probably from a 9mm. At first glance, there didn't appear to be any ligature marks or bruising on her body. Judging by the smell, they had been here for a few days.

She had been a gorgeous woman when she was alive. Even dead, she still had a radiance about her. The long-haired brunette once had piercing blue eyes. Her petite figure was now rapidly decaying.

The camera flashed as Phil began documenting the scene.

"Do we have IDs for the victims?" I asked.

"The boat is registered to Nina Harlow," the petty officer said from the hallway.

JD's eyes rounded. "I'll be damned. That is her."

My eyes narrowed at the woman's corpse. "You're right."

"I should have known from the name of the boat," JD said.

"What about the guy?" I asked.

A pile of clothes lay on the deck. There were frilly lace panties and a black bra. Not far away, a pair of cargo shorts lay crumpled in a haphazard manner near a T-shirt.

Brenda dug into a pocket and pulled a black leather wallet from the shorts. She flipped it open and looked at the man's ID. "Sebastian Simonton."

The name didn't ring a bell.

I spotted several shell casings on the floor. I nudged Phil and had him take photographs. I snapped on a pair of nitrile gloves and waited for the evidence to be chronicled. They were 124 grain, 9mm rounds.

"You guys know the girl?" Brenda asked.

"Well, not personally," JD said. "But I know *of* her."

"Is she somebody famous?"

"You don't know who Nina Harlow is?"

"Should I?"

JD's face twisted. "She's like the biggest thing on the Internet, next to me, of course," he said without a hint of modesty. "She's got the #1-rated podcast. *Dirty talk*."

"That doesn't really sound like my kind of show," Brenda said. "Is it as lurid as it sounds?"

"She's a former porn star turned sex therapist," JD continued. "She does a live show, and people call in with questions about their sex life, dating, etc. It's really great. You would not believe some of the questions people ask. I try to catch just about every episode."

"Figures you would be a fan," Brenda said.

"Man, this is a total bummer. She was smoking hot, too." He thought for a second. "She dated that guy from that band for a while…" JD's face twisted as he tried to recall the name.

"Guess she's not dating him anymore," Brenda said dryly.

JD shot her a look. "Nina was a very intelligent woman," he said, defending her. "She got her Ph.D. and was licensed. She did couples counseling, that kind of thing. She was a sex coach, and people gave rave reviews about how Nina saved their marriages and improved their sex lives. She even had a line of sex toys. I'll bet you anything that dildo in her mouth is one of hers."

Phil snapped close-up pictures of the silicone device.

We stepped to the bed and leaned in for a closer look. The putrid stench intensified.

"You gotta sell a lot of dildos to afford a boat like this," JD muttered, looking for a logo on the base of the rubber dong.

6

"I'd estimate 48 hours, give or take," Brenda said. "I'll know more when I get back to the lab."

"Did Nina see patients on her boat?" Daniels asked.

"If I recall correctly, yes," JD said. "She saw patients here, did all of her podcasts and videos here." In a low voice, he said, "I heard crazy stories about these couples cruises she offered. Designed to promote intimacy and spontaneity. I bet Nina could spice things up."

Brenda shot us an annoyed glance.

"Looks like a crime of passion to me," the Sheriff said. "You don't defile a body like that unless you have strong feelings toward the victim."

I moved back to the hatch and faced the compartment, trying to put myself into the shoes of the killer. "The killer comes in, catches them in the act. They're startled. Sebastian climbs off the bed, and the killer puts two into his chest. He falls to the deck. Then the killer shoots Nina twice. The bullets entered on the right side of her chest like she was reaching for the nightstand. The blood splatter on the sheets confirms it." I moved back to the bed and pulled open the drawer of the nightstand. Sure enough, there was a small 9mm pistol. "You can tell by the bloodstains that the killer repositioned her, spread her arms and legs, then stuffed the, uh... dong... in her mouth."

"Do you think the shooter was already on the boat?" JD asked.

"Let's check to see if the tender is missing. Otherwise, it's possible that someone followed them out here, boarded the boat, and shot them."

"Why don't you contact that reporter friend of yours," Daniels said to me. "Let's get the word out and see if anybody was in the area during the time of the shooting. We know we've got a leak in the department and she's gonna find out anyway. Might as well give her the story straight up and score some brownie points."

"Oh, Tyson can give it to her straight up, all right," JD joked.

My eyes narrowed at him.

JD raised his hands in surrender.

"I'm gonna say jealous boyfriend," Daniels said.

"Or obsessed fan," JD added.

"Where were you 48 hours ago?" Daniels asked him, deadpan.

JD sneered back at him.

"What about pirates?" the petty officer asked. "We've had several reports of thefts at sea lately."

"I don't think so," I said.

A diamond bracelet sparkled around Nina's wrist, and diamond earrings dangled from her delicate lobes.

"The valuables would be gone," I said.

A forensics guy held up a couple diamond necklaces he pulled from the dresser drawer. "She's got a considerable amount of jewelry here. If it's all real, it's worth a small fortune."

"Can you get prints off that sex toy," the sheriff asked.

"I can try," Brenda said. "Hopefully, we'll be able to pull something off the shell casings."

"Let's dust all the handles and surfaces between here and the swim platform. The killer had to touch something on his way in or out."

"He may have been wearing gloves," I said.

"Maybe we'll get lucky," Daniels replied.

We stepped outside the compartment and let Brenda and the forensics team do their thing without distraction. JD and I searched the rest of the boat. The tender was still in the garage.

I called Denise and asked her to pull up information on Nina and Sebastian Simonton. I searched the Internet as well and found quite a few juicy tidbits and a lot of sultry photographs of Nina Harlow from her days as an adult film star. When she was alive, the luscious vixen had smoldering eyes and a rock-solid figure.

Her website featured her podcast, video series, and merchandise that included her two best-selling novels, *Pure Passion* and *99 Ways to Rekindle the Flame*. There was a best-selling line of sex toys and lubricants, naughty lingerie, and a video course on better sex.

Nina had built herself a small empire, and it had all come crashing down.

She was the kind of woman that men would do stupid things for. One look into those smoky eyes, one kiss from those pouty lips, and you'd be hooked. I began to think this wasn't a crime of passion as much as it was a crime of obsession.

When Brenda and the forensics team wrapped up, we helped load the bodies onto the patrol boat. They were sealed in black zippered bags with reinforced carry handles.

The Coast Guard handed off the investigation to us and went about their way. JD and I stayed aboard *Dirty Talk* and piloted the vessel back to Coconut Key. It was a crime scene, and Sheriff Daniels wanted to maintain full control until we got a better handle on this thing.

JD took the helm, and we cruised across the water. It was a beautiful day—sunny and 74 degrees. There was a reason northerners flocked to the island paradise during the winter months.

I could tell that JD was preoccupied with the crime. A sorrowful frown tugged his lips. "That's just a damn shame. I never met her, but I sure did get a kick out of her show."

It wasn't long before we pulled into the marina at the station. I tied off the lines and connected power and water for good measure. We sealed the boat with yellow police tape and put stickers over the sliding glass door that read: *crime scene do not enter*.

We ambled down the dock toward the station. I saw a news van in the parking lot, and Paris Delaney marched toward us with a cameraman and a sound guy. The crew trotted along, trying to keep up with the vivacious blonde.

I didn't have to leak the information to the press. Somebody had already done it for me.

Paris's blonde hair shimmered in the sunlight, and her blue eyes sparkled. She wore a red blazer and a short skirt that revealed her delectable thighs. Her high heels clacked against the dock.

The cameraman focused the lens on me, and the sound man swung the boom mic overhead—the fluffy windscreen hung just out of frame.

"Deputy Wild, what can you tell us about the murders?"

"At this time, we are not releasing the names of the deceased until the next of kin have been notified. But we are asking anyone who has been in the vicinity of *Eel Key* in the last few days to contact the Sheriff's Department if they have seen anything suspicious."

"I see that you've just impounded *Dirty Talk*. That boat belongs to Nina Harlow. Did the murders occur aboard her boat? Is Nina deceased?"

I grimaced. Paris would do anything to break a story.

7

"I can't discuss any details at this time," I said, then continued toward the station.

Paris was a little miffed. Her face scrunched, and I could feel her eyes burn into my back as I walked toward the main doors. She finished her segment, and we stepped inside and found Denise at her desk. Her manicured fingers clacked away at the keyboard. The gorgeous redhead greeted us with a smile, and her emerald eyes pierced into me and stole my breath. "I think you'll be interested in this."

"I'm all ears," I said.

The office buzzed with activity. Phones rang, citizens filed stolen property reports, offenders were processed and printed. The aroma of stale coffee filled the air. Shafts of light beamed through the blinds.

It was a typical day.

"Sebastian Simonton was a tech entrepreneur," Denise said. "He was partnered with a guy named Knox Murphy. They developed a new dating app called *Soulmate*. Last year they got an infusion of $162 million in venture capital."

JD and I raised impressed eyebrows.

"It gets better. I found an article online that said the company just inked a deal to sell the app for $1 billion to *Instabook*."

We stood there, slack-jawed. $1 billion was a lot of money. I shared a glance with JD, and we both were thinking the same thing.

"I'm not so sure Nina was the target," JD said.

"You might want to have a talk with Sebastian's business partner," Denise suggested.

"Can you look up his information?" I asked.

Denise smiled. "I already did. I'll text it to your phone."

"You're the best," I said with a smile.

"I know," she said in her adorable way with an innocent shrug.

"Better notify the next of kin ASAP. That information is about to be public knowledge when Paris broadcasts her segment."

Denise's pretty face crinkled with disdain. "That woman," she said in a huff.

I thanked Denise, and we left the main office and headed toward the parking lot.

"Before we get into this, I need to get something to eat," JD said. He looked at his watch. "I've got the show at *Sonic*

Temple tonight. I need to get to the studio, help the guys load up, and get the gear to the venue. Then we have a quick soundcheck before the doors open."

"What time do you go on?" I asked.

"Not until later. 11 PM." A mischievous grin curled his face. "I've got a little surprise for the guys. They're gonna love this."

I could only imagine what he had in store.

Paris and her news crew still lingered in the parking lot. She trotted toward us as we marched to Jack's Porsche. She came alone, no cameraman in tow. "Hey, off the record..."

I gave her a skeptical glance. Nothing was ever truly off the record with Paris.

"It doesn't take a rocket scientist to put two and two together," she said.

"Then why ask?"

"So Nina was murdered?"

"We will either confirm or deny that shortly," I said.

"I really liked her show," Paris said with a slight frown. "She was fun, spunky, and outrageous. I hope you have some leads."

"We're working on it." I climbed into the Porsche and pulled the door shut.

"Let me know if there's anything I can do to help," Paris said.

I smiled. "Just get the word out that we're looking for potential witnesses."

Jack cranked up the engine, and I buckled my safety harness.

"See you around, Deputy," Paris said, wiggling her fingers as we pulled out of the parking space.

Jack sped out of the lot, and the engine howled.

We cruised to *Mama Maya's* and were quickly seated by a cute hostess. The smell of grilled meat, beans, and jalapeños filled the air. It was one of the best Mexican food restaurants on the island. The place was always packed for lunch and dinner, but we were here at an off-hour, and the crowd was considerably thinner. The building was made of stone and had a Spanish tile roof. Inside, the walls were painted with bright festive colors—teal green, red, and amber.

There was no need to look at the menu. We knew what we wanted. Beef fajitas. Quick and easy.

We relaxed for a moment as the waitress collected our menus and returned shortly with a bowl of gooey queso and warm chips. We crunched away on the highly caloric snack. But it was worth every cheesy bite.

It didn't take long for a sizzling tray of beef to arrive at the table, popping and crackling. The delightful smell of spices wafted through the air. The cast-iron plate contained grilled onions and jalapeños beside the tender strips of beef. The meal was served with sides of Spanish rice, refried beans, guacamole, sour cream, shredded cheese, and pico de gallo.

The margaritas here were lethal. They came in large glasses with blue lips, rimmed with salt. We decided to forgo the tangy infusions of tequila for the moment. We still had work to do.

We packed all the goods into oversized flour tortillas, drenched them with cheese, rolled them up, and stuffed our mouths. Taste buds exploded with sensory overload.

"So, what's this surprise for the band?" I asked with a mouthful.

"Just a little something we need. Plus, I want to show the guys that I am 100% committed to *Wild Fury*."

"So you're turning down the offer to go on tour with..."

"Yep."

"That must have been a tough one."

"Yup," JD said.

"I think you made the right decision."

"I gotta say, I thought about it for a minute. Fronting one of the biggest rock bands in history is hard to say no to. But it would have been detrimental to *Wild Fury*. I think we can make our own mark."

"I have no doubt." I paused. "So, what's the surprise?"

JD grinned again. "You'll see." He paused. "Speaking of the band, we need to shoot the next video."

"I'm down whenever."

"I'm thinking next weekend. I can get the film school guys back. We'll knock it out just like last time. Except, we'll be a little more careful with the gear." His accusatory eyes blazed into me.

I raised my hands in surrender. "That won't happen again." I took another bite, then asked, "Any ideas for this one?"

"Nope. I'm leaving that up to you. You're the director. You come up with the concept. You did last time, and it worked. Why change a winning team?"

"No pressure," I said.

"There's something else I want to talk to you about."

"Shoot," I said, encouraging him to continue.

"Later," he said.

I wondered what was up his sleeve, but figured I'd find out soon enough.

We devoured the meal in no time.

Brenda called just as we were finishing up. "I'm gonna revise my estimate. Judging by the stage of insect larva, I'm going to put the time of death between 7 and 10 PM Wednesday night."

Insect larva wasn't exactly what I wanted to think about while staring at a plate of Spanish rice. "Thanks, that's helpful."

"Also, I don't believe the victim was sexually assaulted, other than the placement of the sex toy, which was definitely put in her mouth after death."

"Anything else?"

"No prints on the sex toy or shell casings. Our killer was smart and wore gloves."

My face tightened with disappointment.

"The bullets are jacketed hollow points. I'll run ballistics on the slugs, see if they are a match for anything in our system."

"Keep me posted," I said. I thanked Brenda for the information and ended the call.

JD signaled the waitress, and she brought the check. He stuffed a wad of cash in the leather folio, leaving a fat tip. We left the restaurant, our bellies full. Jack gave a quick glance to his watch and said, "Let's go talk to Knox."

8

The *Soulmates* office looked more like the rec room of a college dorm than it did a company valued at $1 billion. There were beanbag chairs, a pool table, a foosball table, two videogame stations with large flatscreen displays—one of which had a full-on racing seat, steering wheel, gear shifter, and pedals. The furniture was sleek and modern. There were sit/stand desks, fully loaded 27-inch iMac's, and downtempo ambient music filtering through surround speakers. Floor-to-ceiling windows offered a view of the ocean a few blocks away. It didn't seem like a lot of work was getting done, but there were a few people diligently clacking away at computer terminals.

I expected to see more employees in a billion-dollar company, but there were less than a dozen, and all of them looked barely out of high school. There was no formal reception desk. This wasn't a place that saw many visitors. This was the backend of a social app.

A young girl saw us standing awkwardly, scoping out the place. She had long, straight, raven hair. She approached and asked, "Can I help you?"

JD flashed his badge. "We're looking for Knox Murphy."

She hesitated, and concern filled her brown eyes. "Uh, yeah. He's right over there. She pointed across the open floor plan to a private office in the corner.

We thanked her, and she went about her way, gossiping with her colleagues as we strolled across the room toward Knox's office. His office was separated with floor to ceiling glass. Knox sat at a desk, talking to someone on his phone through Airpods. We knocked on the glass door, then pulled it open.

"Hang on a second," he said, looking perturbed at our intrusion.

JD flashed his badge again before Knox could ask who we were.

He had a boyish face and couldn't have been more than 22. Unlike the other office workers, Knox wore a suit but no tie. His brown hair was stylishly shaggy, and his bangs fell to his eyebrows. He was handsome in a geeky kind of way. The *Joubert* watch on his wrist, and designer *Di Fiore* suit, told me he had expensive taste.

"I'll need to call you back," he muttered. Knox ended the call but didn't bother to pull the earbuds from his ears. The young CEO forced a smile. "What can I do for you, gentlemen?"

"I'm afraid we have some disappointing news," I said.

I told him that his business partner had been murdered.

His jaw dropped and his eyes rounded. "Are you serious?"

I nodded.

He took a moment to process the information, then stammered, "What happened?"

I get concerned when people don't ask how a person died. Guilty people already know. Either he put on a good show, or he was genuinely curious. I filled him in on the general details.

Knox slumped and exhaled as it sunk in.

"Can you tell me where you were Wednesday evening?" I asked.

Knox's face twisted while he thought. "I was at home with my wife. Why?"

"Just curious. And your wife's name is?"

"Makenna," he said.

"I'll need her contact information."

"Sure. Do you have any leads?"

"We have several avenues to pursue," I said.

Knox looked dazed. He shook his head, "I can't believe this."

"When was the last time you spoke with Sebastian?"

"Tuesday, I think."

"And it didn't concern you that he went missing for a few days?"

"No. We just closed the deal on Monday. Sebastian said he was going to take a few days off and spend time with Nina."

"How long had they been dating?"

He sucked his teeth, then blew out a breath. "I guess a month or two?"

"Was it serious?"

Knox scoffed. "The word serious and Sebastian don't really belong in the same sentence. I think they were just having fun. Seb liked to have fun."

"Seems like he was on top of the world."

"Yeah, amazing things are happening with the company. This is just terrible."

"Tell me a little bit about the app," I said.

"It's been a project we've worked on since college. We came up with the concept—I did all the programming, Sebastian handled the business side of things. He was good with people and funding. He got us the venture capital. He put together the deal with *Instabook*. This company wouldn't be anywhere without him. I don't know what we're gonna do or what this means for the future." The magnitude of the situation began to sink in.

"Does the app work? You make some pretty lofty claims," I said.

"What can I say... It absolutely works. It's how I met my wife. And we are a perfect fit."

"How long have you been married?"

"Six months."

JD and I exchanged a glance. Not near enough time to establish proof of compatibility.

"So, how does the match system work?" JD asked.

"It's a simple concept, really. Everybody that signs up to the platform fills out a specifically designed questionnaire about their likes, dislikes, political affiliations, sexual preferences, pet peeves, you name it. Some questions are more important than others, and we tend to ask the same questions in multiple ways, trying to get honest answers. People tend to lie and make themselves sound better than they actually are. But the questionnaire is just one small piece of the puzzle. The main compatibility measures are scraped from multiple databases and the Internet. The app searches through social media profiles and posts, credit history, voting record, and numerous other data sources which I can't reveal, to put together a complete profile. Then we have a specifically designed predictive modeling algorithm that will align people with common interests and rate them on compatibility. Are they looking for a good time? Are they looking to settle down and start a family? It really works."

"With Seb gone, who assumes his share of the company?"

"I don't really know," Knox said. "I'd have to talk to the lawyers. We sold the majority interest but maintained a percentage. The venture capital guys got bought out. We have a contract to stay on for five years. I'm not sure how this all works out without Seb."

"What about life insurance?" I asked.

"I know the VC guys had a business policy that if either of the principles died, they would recoup."

"What was the dollar amount?"

"I'd have to check, but it was enough to cover their full investment. But it's a moot point now that the company has sold."

"What about you? Did you have a policy as well?"

"Honestly, it never crossed my mind. I didn't think one of us would get murdered."

"Still, you've amassed a considerable fortune."

"Yes, I have. And I see where you're going with this. Sebastian was a friend. I had no incentive to murder him because I've already made more money than I could ever spend in five lifetimes."

"What about disgruntled co-workers or exes?" I asked.

Knox's eyes brightened. "Now that's where you need to be looking."

JD and I exchanged a curious glance.

"At whom, in particular?"

9

"**Y**ou need to talk to Heidi," Knox said. "That chick is certifiable."

"How so?" I asked.

"She went completely psycho on Seb. I mean, she seemed nice enough at first, then it was like a switch flipped. I always got a strange vibe from her, even from the beginning. When she gets mad, forget about it. She had those serial killer eyes. It was like she became possessed." He shivered. "They had only hooked up a couple of times, and she was ready to lock that shit down. I get it. Sebastian was a good-looking guy. He always did well with the ladies. Plus, he was rolling in dough. I mean, what girl wouldn't want to make that guy her forever home? I told him something was a little off about Heidi, but, you know how it is, he had to do it anyway."

"How long did they date?"

"I wouldn't even call it dating. They hooked up a couple of times over the course of maybe a month. She was already talking about getting married and having kids. When Sebastian cut that off, she totally flipped out."

"What did she do?"

"Called and texted him all the time. Nonstop. One minute she would call him every name in the book, and the next, she'd send a flurry of texts apologizing. Weird."

"How long ago did they stop seeing each other?" I asked.

"I don't know... Maybe 4 or 5 months ago."

"Have they seen each other since?"

Knox hesitated. "I don't think so. But I don't think Seb would admit to me if he hooked up with her again."

"So, it's safe to say you didn't like her," I said, stating the obvious.

"I told Seb to steer clear of her. Don't get me wrong, she's hot as fuck, but the juice isn't worth the squeeze." He thought for a moment. "I remember we were out one night, and he told her straight up that they were just hanging out and having fun and not to get any ideas about a relationship. And she lied and said she knew it was just casual. Heidi would say whatever she thought he wanted to hear."

"That doesn't make her a murderer," I said.

"Well, I'm telling you she should be a person of interest. The girl is unstable."

"Did she ever get violent?"

"Yeah, I guess you could say that. She'd get mad and smack him. And when he cut it off, she keyed his Ferrari."

JD winced.

"And I'm not talking light scratches that buff out. I'm talking down to the metal."

"Did Sebastian file a police report?"

"No. He just let it slide. He didn't want to antagonize her. He figured it would die down given enough time."

"Did the harassment stop?"

"As far as I knew. I think she sent him a few shitty texts when she found out that he was hooking up with Nina Harlow."

"How did Sebastian meet Nina?"

"It's kinda funny. Seb called into her show and said he had a crush on a girl but was too shy to act. Nina told him to just go for it and ask the girl out. Life is short. So Seb told Nina he thought she was hot and asked her out. Kinda put her on the spot. She said she didn't date random callers. Seb said he was rich. Nina asked how rich? Seb said *very*. Nina said she would agree to a date if he donated a million dollars to her preferred charity. I guess she thought that would get rid of him, but Seb coughed up the dough." Knox sighed. "I guess that was the worst money he ever spent. Maybe he'd still be alive if he didn't hook up with her."

"Do you happen to have Heidi's contact information?"

"No. But I'm sure you guys can figure it out." Knox told me Heidi's last name, and I sent a text to Denise asking her to look up the girl's information.

"Can you think of anyone else that may have wanted to harm Sebastian? Business associates, competitors, rivals?"

Knox thought for a long moment. "No. I really can't. Sebastian was a likable kind of guy. But that is one thing about success... you stay the same, but a lot of people around you start to change. They have certain expectations, and everybody seems to want something from you. People you haven't talked to in years show up asking for favors. It's kind of crazy. People you thought were your friends can start to hate you real quick. Jealousy is a strange thing, man."

Knox gave me his wife's cell phone number. I called Makenna while we were in his office, and she verified his alibi, which is exactly what I expected her to do.

I gave Knox my card and told him we might be in touch. We left his office, and he prepared to make an announcement to the rest of the staff. He stepped out of his office and called his employees to gather around as we left the office and walked to the elevators.

JD pressed the call button.

"You think we have time to track down Heidi before you need to get to the practice studio?" I asked.

He looked at his watch. "I think we can squeeze her in."

The doors slid open. We stepped onto the elevator and descended to the first-floor lobby. Denise texted me a moment later with Heidi's contact information.

10

K nox was right. Heidi seemed really nice. She had a sweet, innocent voice that was breathy and soft. She had flawless, creamy skin, and her long natural lashes fluttered about her crystal blue eyes. Her blonde hair shimmered and fell to her shoulders like a waterfall of gold. Her petite little form drew the eye. She was the girl-next-door—someone you wanted to take home and meet the family, at least until her dark side came out.

She worked at a pet store and cradled an adorable white kitten in her arms when we found her. She was in an aisle with a row of kennels on one side and supplies on the other. Parakeets chirped in their cages, dogs barked, fish tanks bubbled, and the air smelled like pet food, fur, and poop.

We flashed our badges and made introductions.

Heidi's eyes rounded, and she shifted uncomfortably.

"We'd like to ask you a few questions about Sebastian Simonton," I said.

"Wow, that name is a blast from the past," she said, dramatically. "I haven't seen Sebastian in a long time."

"I wouldn't exactly call a few months a *blast from the past*," I said.

"Well, it's ancient history as far as I'm concerned."

"Can you tell me a little about your relationship?"

She shrugged nonchalantly. "There's not much to tell. It wasn't much of a relationship."

"So, you were just casually dating?"

"That's how I look at it. But Sebastian got a little... attached. Don't get me wrong, he's a nice guy and all, but he just got way too obsessive."

"Really?" I asked with a slightly incredulous tone.

"He was *really* needy," she said, almost in a groan. "He wanted to spend every waking hour with me." She flipped her hair. "I told him from the beginning we were just having fun, but he was ready to settle down. He didn't want me seeing anybody else. I think he was about to propose, honestly."

Somebody was lying. "Is that so?"

"I don't know. I just seem to have that effect on men. I don't know what it is." Heidi paused. "Why? What has he done?" Her eyes widened, and she gasped as a horrible thought filled her mind. "He's not stalking someone else, is he? He hasn't killed anyone, has he?"

"No. I'm sorry to say that Sebastian is dead."

Her jaw dropped, and she gasped again. In an overly dramatic fashion, she covered her mouth and teared up. "Are you serious?"

"Yes, ma'am. I'm sorry to be the bearer of bad news."

"Oh, my God, that is so freaky! I just had a dream the other day that he was dead."

"Really?" I asked, curious.

She waved it away with her hand. "I dismissed it as nonsense. I almost thought about calling him to see if he was okay, but I didn't want to start anything up again."

"Tell me more about your dream."

"I don't know, it was weird. I dreamt he got shot."

JD and I exchanged a glance.

She noted the exchange. "Why? Did he get shot?"

"Do you own a pistol?"

She hesitated, then nodded. "Yeah, why?"

"Why do you own a pistol?"

"Because it's my right. And for self-defense. It's crazy out there. And I'm cute," she said in an adorable voice. "Sometimes when I close up at the store, it's 10 PM, and the parking lot can be a scary place."

"Do you have the pistol with you now?"

She nodded, still stroking the cute little kitty. "It's in my purse by the register."

"Do you mind if we see it?"

She hesitated for a moment. "I don't see why not."

She put the little kitty back in a kennel with the others, then we followed her to the front desk.

"Is anyone else working here today?" I asked.

"No, it's just me today. It's been pretty slow lately." She dug into her purse and pulled out a 9mm and set it on the counter. "It's loaded, by the way. I have a concealed weapon license."

"Can I see your license?"

"Sure." She dug into her purse again.

Heidi handed the license to me, and I looked it over.

You had to have a pretty spotless record to get a concealed weapon license. You needed to pass a background check and demonstrate proficiency with a firearm. The fact that she had been able to acquire one told me she didn't have much of note in her background.

I examined the weapon, press-checked it, and sniffed the barrel. It was loaded with 124 grain hollow-points and had been fired recently.

"I just went to the range a few days ago. Gotta keep up the skills."

"You go often?"

"Once a week. I love shooting." She closed her eyes and breathed through her nostrils, reliving the sensation. "The smell of gunpowder. The feeling of something powerful in your hand. The bang!" She opened her eyes on the verge of ecstasy. "It's addictive. You know what I'm talking about, right? It's almost as good as sex." A mischievous glint flickered in her deceptively innocent eyes. *"Almost."*

"Do you mind if we take this to the lab and run some tests?" I asked.

11

Heidi's delicate face twisted into a snarl. I saw a flash of the demon in her eyes. "I do mind. And I don't appreciate your accusatory tone."

"Where were you Wednesday evening?" I asked.

Her eyes continued to blaze into me. "Right here! Working till 10 PM," she snapped. "I'm sorry, but I'm not rich like Sebastian. I have to work for a living."

"Was anybody else working with you at the time?"

"No. Just me and the animals."

I pressed the mag release and dropped the magazine into my palm. I set it on the counter, then ejected the round from the chamber. I caught it in the air before it hit the ground. I set the weapon on the counter along with the bullet.

"You own a boat?" I asked.

"I'm not answering any more questions."

I frowned. With a mild dose of sarcasm, I said, "Thanks for your cooperation."

JD and I left the blonde in the pet shop. A parrot cackled as we pushed through the exit door, "Have a nice day!"

JD muttered, "She went from nice to nasty real quick."

With a voice full of skepticism, I asked, "Do you buy her story about Sebastian stalking her?"

JD shrugged. "I don't think Sebastian was hurting for options."

We hopped into the Porsche and cruised to JD's house. He pulled into the circular drive, and I got a view of his surprise for the guys.

I had a good chuckle. It was so insane.

A matte black muscle van from the '70s crouched in the driveway, ready to spring into action. It was lowered, had fat tires, and polished chrome Crager S/S rims. Massive chrome exhaust pipes ran along the sides, and the *Wild Fury* logo was painted on the side panels, complete with skull and sword. The van even had the classic bubble porthole windows in the rear sides. It was a beast and the ideal vehicle to haul around the band's equipment from gig to gig.

I was stunned. "Oh, my God! Where did you get that thing?"

"I picked it up on an auction site, then had it completely rebuilt by *Coconut Customs*. All new interior, new engine, custom paint. The thing has got like 600 hp!"

We hopped out of the Porsche and walked around Jack's new toy. I marveled at the creation. The front grill had been custom made to resemble shark's teeth. The bodywork and paint were flawless.

JD clicked the alarm, and I pulled open the passenger door. The interior did not disappoint. There were diamond-stitched leather seats and matching floor mats. The dashboard had been completely redone with hand-stitched leather. The air conditioning vents were brushed aluminum, and they looked like exhausts on fighter jets. Of course, the thing had a bumping stereo system with massive speakers. White fuzzy dice hung from the mirror, and a chrome silhouette of a buxom pinup adorned the center console. The racing-style Alcantara steering wheel and all-new gauges almost made it feel like the cockpit of a fighter jet. The gas pedal was in the shape of a bare footprint in classic '70s fashion.

The cargo compartment had a removable row of leather seats, and behind that, space for drums, guitars, and amp cabinets. There was no faux wood paneling in this '70s era van. No shag carpet. It was upholstered with leather and brushed aluminum panels. It was part throwback, part futuristic. It was a machine that could transport you to another dimension.

JD hopped behind the wheel and twisted the ignition. The engine growled, and JD pumped the gas. The exhaust rumbled, and the pistons screamed. Even sitting still, the van felt like it could launch to the moon.

JD had a wide grin on his face. "What do you think? Think the guys will like it?"

I smiled. "I think they'll love it."

"Hop in. Let's take her for a spin."

I climbed into the passenger seat and pulled the door shut. It smelled like fresh leather and oil. The van vibrated as the engine snarled and chimed. It echoed down the block and was the kind of sound that would piss off the neighbors if you started it up too early in the morning or came home too late at night.

JD put the van into gear and rolled out of the driveway. He held back as we cruised down the street, but he was just dying to stand on the pedal. As soon as we turned out of the neighborhood, he stomped on the gas.

The engine howled, and the tires spun. The van stood still as white smoke billowed from the wheel wells. Tires squealed as they put down a thick black streak on the pavement.

After he'd burned through enough rubber, he let off the gas and smiled. The noxious smoke drifted away on the breeze. "How ya like them apples?"

12

The roar of the engine echoed off the buildings in the warehouse district. We rolled through the industrial part of town and pulled into the parking lot at the rehearsal studio. JD found a spot close to the entrance.

It was a dodgy part of town, and the cars in the lot looked like veterans of a demolition derby—crappy vans and cheap imports with dented quarter-panels and patchworks of Bondo. Most musicians didn't have two nickels to rub together—a situation made worse by the ever decreasing royalty payouts and downward pressure on fees that live bands could command.

Wild Fury's old van sagged in the lot, ready to be put out to pasture. It had its fair share of dents, scrapes, and rust spots.

The usual group of metalheads and stoners hung out by the entrance to the practice hall. They wore lots of leather and studded belts. Black fingernail polish and heavy eyeliner. Their red eyes widened when they saw the new van.

We hopped out and strolled toward the entrance.

"Awesome! Totally awesome!" a kid said, squinting through long black hair that fell into his eyes. He high-fived JD.

We pushed inside and made our way down the corridor that smelled like a combination of fresh herb and incense. The rumble of other bands practicing seeped through the walls.

We pushed into *Wild Fury's* practice studio, and the guys were prepping their gear. Dizzy and Crash packed their guitars in cases. Styxx broke down his candy apple red drum set. There were glum faces all around.

"Dude, we have a major problem," Styxx said.

JD's face crinkled. "What is it?"

"We'll have to rent a moving van or something. Our van won't start."

JD shook his head dismissively. "Not an issue."

Styxx's brow knitted together. "What do you mean, *not an issue?*"

"I have it all taken care of." Jack smiled.

The guys looked perplexed.

JD kept the secret while we helped them pack up. We loaded the gear onto a dolly and began making trips to the van. When the band stepped outside, they didn't notice the new vehicle at first and started hauling the gear toward the old van.

"Where the hell are you going?" JD asked.

Styxx looked at him, perplexed.

JD pointed to the new vehicle. "Open your eyes."

Jaws dropped, and eyes bulged from sockets.

"Holy shit!" Styxx uttered, awestruck.

JD grinned.

"Where the hell did that come from?" Dizzy asked.

"Just a little something I've been working on." JD escorted them to the van and gave them a tour. He clicked the alarm, pulled open the doors, and cranked up the engine, giving them a little taste of the snarling beast.

There were astonished smiles all around, and the guys in the band gawked at their new transportation, which also served as an advertisement for the band.

"I guess this means you're sticking around," Styxx said.

"Did you really think I'd leave you guys and go on tour with another band?" JD asked.

The guys exchanged a look and said in unison, "Yeah."

JD scowled at them playfully. "No way! We are all in this together. In it to win it. It's *Wild Fury* or bust."

That put smiles on their faces. They all high-fived each other, then continued to load the vehicle. We made a few trips and stuffed all the gear aboard, then crammed inside and headed over to the venue.

Sonic Temple was the premier rock venue on Oyster Avenue. Home to local bands and touring national acts, it had become a regular spot for *Wild Fury.* They headlined every few weeks.

JD pulled the van into the parking lot behind the club and killed the engine. The band spilled out and began loading their gear inside and prepared for a sound check. It was still daylight by the time they finished, but the sun was plummeting toward the horizon.

We left the venue, and JD took the band out for a pre-show meal. The guys wanted steaks, so Jack treated them to *Cowtown*. It was a family restaurant where you could get sirloins, fillets, ribeyes, mesquite grilled burgers, spicy curly fries, baked potatoes with all the fixings, and a host of side dishes like mac & cheese, sautéed mushrooms, green beans, and fried onions. It was Western themed with cedar plank walls and black and white pictures of longhorns.

We kicked around a few ideas for the next music video. After the success of the last one, the band didn't put up much of an argument about the direction JD wanted to take it.

The steaks were tender and juicy, and the guys put them away like they hadn't eaten in days. *They might not have.* Even with the success of the last video, and the millions of streams, the royalties hadn't trickled in yet. And when they did, the band would only receive small fractions of a cent per stream—and that was keeping 100% of the royalties as independent artists. The deals were worse for signed artists that gave away up to 92% of their royalties.

Jack had set up an LLC for the band and handled all the finances, tracking expenses and revenue. They had yet to make a profit, but that was about to change when the royalties from *All I Need* were deposited into the account. It wasn't about the money, anyway.

"So, there's some business I'd like to discuss," JD said in a serious tone.

The table quieted, and all eyes fell on JD.

"I've talked to the guys, and we all agree," Jack said to me. "We want you to be our manager."

Surprise washed over my face. My eyes flicked from JD to the rest of the guys for confirmation. JD had occasionally referred to me as their manager when speaking with groupies. I figured it was his way of including me in the band and conveying some of the enigmatic magic that the band held in the eyes of adoring groupies. But I never took it seriously.

"Yeah, man," Styxx said. "You knocked it out of the park with the video, and it was a good call creatively."

"I'm flattered, but I've never managed a band before. I don't know anything about it. Are you sure? You guys have had offers from real managers with real connections."

"We trust you," Styxx said. "And that's all that matters."

"I don't even know what to do," I said.

"Neither do any of us," Dizzy said. "We'll all learn as we go."

"As this thing gets bigger, I'm gonna need help coordinating shows, handling merchandise, and overseeing marketing," JD said. "We want to bring you on as a full partner. 1/5th of everything."

I lifted an impressed brow. "That's very generous."

"It's not generous. It's fair," JD said. "It's going to be a lot of work."

"You need to look after us," Crash said. "Keep us on track. Keep us from getting fucked by sleazy promoters and too fucked up on party favors."

It was a huge responsibility. "I'm really honored guys. But I need to think about it. I certainly don't want to let you down."

"If we thought there was a possibility of you letting us down, we wouldn't have asked," Styxx said.

I paused for a long moment. There was no telling these guys no. "I guess I'm your manager."

There were smiles and cheers all around. We all lifted our glasses and toasted to the new partnership. I hoped I wasn't biting off more than I could chew.

After we filled our bellies, we tabbed out, left *Cowtown,* and headed back to Oyster Avenue. JD parked the van at *Sonic Temple.* It was early, and the band wouldn't go on for several hours. The guys decided to kill the time at *Blackbeards,* and we made the short walk down the block.

It was a pirate themed bar built to look like a galleon with heavy cannons, shrouds, masts, and riggings. There were barrels of rum, and the cocktail waitresses wore skimpy little pirate costumes. The bar was a direct competitor to *Mutiny* which had a similar aesthetic. There was a lot of eye candy and it wasn't a bad place to spend a few hours before the show while the band got sufficiently lubricated to go on stage.

Wild Fury had decided not to make themselves too available before shows. They wanted to keep a little mystery about them instead of loitering around *Sonic Temple,* drinking with fans. They'd save that for after the show, but they wanted to build pre-show suspense.

We hung out at *Blackbeard's* for a few hours, then made our way back to *Sonic Temple* around 10:15 PM. The line to get in circled the building, and the rumble of the opening act filtered into the street. The crowd grew larger with each show. There was a lot of teased hair, heavy eyeliner, short skirts, long legs, and stiletto heels. Glossy red lips and low-cut tops that showcased ample cleavage. It was exactly the kind of audience you wanted to see at a rock 'n' roll concert.

We were in for a helluva night.

13

L*ipstick Revolution* finished their set, hauled their gear offstage, and *Wild Fury* set up.

The rockers thundered onto the stage at II PM to roaring fans with hands stretched toward the heavens. They screamed with excitement. Styxx stomped the kick drum. Dizzy struck a power chord, and his guitar growled. Crash plucked his bass, laying down the groove. A wall of amplification pummeled eardrums. JD grabbed the mic and howled, "Are you ready to rock?"

The crowd cheered with enthusiasm.

"I can't hear you?"

They screamed even louder.

"Say what?" Jack held the microphone toward the audience, and they hollered louder still.

Styxx pounded out a fill on the snare drum, and the band broke into the first verse of *Iron Heart.* JD's blistering voice filled the venue.

I hung out and watched the show while Jack pranced around, howling into the mic and flipping his long blond hair in true rockstar fashion. Dizzy and Crash head-banged, grinding out thunderous tones on their axes. Styxx twirled his drumsticks and beat the drums like a madman. Colored lights swirled and slashed the air. Fog billowed from the stage.

By this point in time, *Wild Fury* was a polished act that put on a show worthy of an arena. Girls threw bras and panties on stage. They would flash Dizzy, and he'd toss them guitar picks. It was like Mardi Gras.

A cute little brunette bumped into me on the way to the bar. She was a little obvious about it. I didn't mind. I didn't mind at all.

"I'm sorry," she shouted over the music, pretending like she hadn't done it on purpose. Her eyes brightened with recognition. "Hey, I know you."

I squinted at her, trying to put a name to her pretty face.

"It's Phoebe," she said. "You saved my dog."

"I thought that was you."

How I rescued the little pooch from certain doom was another story altogether.

"I didn't know you were a *Wild Fury* fan," Phoebe said.

"Jack, I mean, *Thrash*, is a friend of mine.

Thrash was JD's stage name.

Her eyes widened. "Really? That's so cool. I'd love to meet him."

"I think that can be arranged," I said with a smirk. "I actually manage the band."

"No way," she said in awe.

"How is Cooper? That's your dog's name, right?"

"You remembered! He's doing well. Hyperactive, but well." Phoebe paused. "I was just going to get a drink. You want something?"

Never one to turn down an offer from a gracious lady, I said, "Whiskey. Rocks."

She smiled. "Coming right up."

Phoebe took my hand and pulled me along as she squeezed her way to the bar. Her hand was soft and warm. It felt nice. I could get used to holding it.

Phoebe had long dark hair and an adorable face. Big beautiful blue eyes, pouty lips, and a petite little figure that she showed off with a leather miniskirt that barely covered anything. Her fishnet stockings and stiletto heels accentuated her divine legs. She had stellar assets.

It didn't take Phoebe long to get the bartender's attention—along with the attention of all the surrounding men—as she leaned against the bar, pushing her cleavage together. She had all-natural, positively buoyant endowments. She ordered our drinks and paid the tab in cash. She handed me my beverage and lifted her glass to toast. "To *Wild Fury*."

I concurred.

We clinked glasses and sipped the fine whiskey. The warm amber liquid swirled around in my mouth, and lustful thoughts swirled in my brain.

We moved away from the bar and found a little space near the rear of the club. The crowd had rushed the stage when *Wild Fury* began to play. Fighting the crowd by the stage took dedication and perseverance. It was hot and sweaty, and you undulated uncontrollably with the rhythm of the crowd, like drifting in a vast ocean. I preferred to hang back and watch the show from a distance. I was glad Phoebe didn't want to dive into the fray.

The perky little brunette grabbed my arm, lifted on her tiptoes, and spoke into my ear. "I'm so glad I ran into you. I thought I might never see you again."

There was an enticing sparkle in her eyes. Her gaze was full of possibilities. Possibilities that I'd like to explore.

"Maybe it's fate," I said.

"Indeed. This is twice fate brought us together."

"I risked my life to save your dog, you know," I said.

She smiled. "I know. How can I ever repay you?"

It was a loaded question.

After the show, the sweaty rockers filed off the stage, and I followed them into the green room, pulling Phoebe along, moving past security. An ice-cold tub of beer, and bottles of whiskey, awaited. The band high-fived each other, toweled off, and celebrated another successful show.

I introduced Phoebe to *Thrash* and the band.

The building vibrated as fans stomped and chanted for an encore. After a quick break, they took the stage again and did another hard-hitting three-song set.

Wild Fury left the stage, then returned again for a second encore to finish the night.

The crowd still continued to chant, even with the house lights on.

There was no shortage of sultry vixens wanting to party with the band—*the perks of rock 'n' roll*. The band broke down their gear and partied with fans at *Sonic Temple* until the bar closed. We loaded the gear into the van, then moved the party back to the *Avventura* as usual.

It was almost 3 AM by the time we got back to the marina at *Diver Down*. The boat was packed with stunning groupies and fans—all going through our stash of beer and liquor at a breakneck pace. Music pumped, and a few of our neighbors joined in the fun.

A few others complained.

We tried to keep the noise to a minimum. But that was like trying to silence a freight train.

It wasn't long before the Jacuzzi on the sundeck was full of naked beauties. Water beaded and glistened on pert bosoms. Bikini bottoms floated among the bubbles and dangled from the ledge.

There were plenty of guys that hung around, trying to pick up girls that weren't receiving the band's full attention. I didn't know half the people here, and the parties grew larger and more insane each time.

Couples paired off and escaped to the guest staterooms to take care of business. Some people didn't even bother to find a private area. On the settee in the salon, a cute blonde had her head buried into a guy's lap, trying to find out just how many licks it took to get to the center of a tootsie pop. Her head bobbed up and down while the dude sipped his beer. Even the fans were living like rock stars at a *Wild Fury* party.

Phoebe seemed shocked by some of the antics. There was a sweet innocence about her. "Is it always like this?"

I shrugged. "It gets a little crazy from time to time."

"I'll say," she said. "You guys must be having the time of your life?"

"You know, life is good," I admitted.

"And this boat," she said, admiring the appointments. "It's fantastic. I could only dream of living on something like this. It must be fun." She looked around. "Obviously, it's fun." She paused. "Why don't you give me a tour?"

"I'd love to." I extended my arm, and she took it.

I led her around the boat and showed her the galley, then took her below deck and gave her a tour of the engine room. The noise and music rumbled above. We were alone for a moment, and I think that was her intention.

"My, what big engines you have," she joked in a naughty voice.

I grinned. "They get the job done."

"I bet."

Her words were wet and slippery. Her blue eyes stared into mine, and her luscious lips beckoned and as she inched closer, never losing eye contact.

I put my hand on the small of her back and pulled her close. Her supple body pressed against mine, and heat radiated. Her soft breath tickled my skin as her lips hovered millimeters away from mine, her sultry eyes piercing into me.

We were about to collide when a couple burst into the compartment. They stumbled in, their lips locked, devouring each other for a moment before they saw us. "Whoops, sorry! Didn't know this was occupied."

The couple giggled and backed out of the compartment.

"Is there somewhere more private we can go?" Phoebe whispered in a voice that took hold of my spine and ignited desire.

14

"This is really nice," Phoebe said upon entering my stateroom.

Located on the bridge deck and spanning the full beam, the compartment was regal. Her eyes took in the lounge area, the luxurious appointments, the flatscreen display that folded down from the ceiling, the queen-size berth.

Buddy barked and bounced, longing for attention. Phoebe knelt down and loved on the little Jack Russell.

He soaked it up.

I pulled the curtains shut, giving us a little privacy. The dull rumble of the party filtered through the bulkheads.

Phoebe stood up and sauntered around the compartment, pretending to check it out before circling back around to me. She slinked toward me like a panther and purred, "Where were we?"

"Right here," I said, pulling her close, finally tasting her sweet lips.

Our tongues danced, and my hands traced every supple curve of her body. We smashed together, exchanging heat. The subtle scent of her shampoo filled my nostrils. Together, we smeared all traces of her cherry lipstick.

Buddy watched, wagging his tail. He eventually got bored and climbed onto a chair in the lounge and curled up.

Phoebe and I stumbled toward the bed and collapsed atop it, our lips locked. It wasn't long before her small leather skirt was above her hips, revealing her frilly lace panties. Our hips mashed together, and we tumbled around the bed.

Things were definitely getting hot and heavy.

My heart pounded, and I came to the firm conclusion that we had too many clothes on. I pulled off my shirt, and she ran her fingers along my chest, her manicured nails lightly grazing my skin. I helped her remove her top. With a well-practiced maneuver, I unclasped her bra. Her glorious orbs sprang free and reaffirmed my belief in a higher power.

Phoebe was gorgeous, and she definitely lit my fuse.

She was an appetizer, a main course, and a dessert all rolled into one. The thrill of anticipation filled me. I wanted to savor every moment, but at the same time, I couldn't wait until there was nothing between us.

"Hey, before this goes too far, I want you to know that I'm not like the girls you're probably used to."

"You're definitely unique," I said, nibbling on her ear.

"I'm having a lot of fun with you. I don't want to stop what we're doing. But I'm not gonna sleep with you tonight."

I grinned. "So you're gonna make me work for it?"

She laughed. "Yeah, a little. If I give it away free, it's not gonna have any value."

"Oh, I'm sure there's plenty of value there," I said.

"Play your cards right, and you might find out."

"I'm a really good card player. Did I mention that?"

"I can tell." She paused. "You're not mad, are you?"

My face scrunched up. "No. I'm not mad. Why would I be? We'll hook up if and when the time is right."

"Believe me, I want to. And the time is right. I'm just not the kind of girl that can jump in the sack right away. Don't get me wrong, I'm not the *wait until marriage type*, but I'm not some floozy either."

"Hey, I'm good with whatever. I'm just enjoying myself."

"I'm glad you're enjoying yourself. I just don't want you to enjoy yourself *too much* and get past the point of no return if you know what I mean."

I laughed. "I appreciate your concern."

"I don't want you to build up pressure that you can't release."

"You're so thoughtful," I snarked.

"It doesn't mean we can't still fool around." She had a hopeful look in her eyes.

"We can still fool around," I said. "It doesn't have to go anywhere."

She smiled. "Good. You're a good kisser. I like kissing you."

"You're not too bad yourself."

She arched a disappointed eyebrow at me. "*Not too bad?*"

"Yeah. Kissing you does not suck."

"Well, I was kind of hoping for something more like *phenomenal, amazing, wonderful...* Those kinds of adjectives."

"Those would all be appropriate."

"I guess, in that case, you can keep kissing me."

I was happy to accept her invitation. Our lips collided again, and we devoured each other. We fooled around for a while, and I tried to temper my enthusiasm, keeping in mind that this would most likely require a cold shower afterward.

It was getting late anyway, and the party was dying down. I'm sure all the guest staterooms were full with the kind of action that I wasn't getting. But I wasn't disappointed. It was actually kind of intriguing. It left a little mystery to things. And the anticipation of pleasure is half the fun.

Phoebe snuggled up to me, and before I dozed off, she kissed me on the cheek and whispered in my ear. "Thanks for understanding. I think you're great."

I dozed off, and all too soon, the morning sun blasted through the windows, beaming shafts of light into the stateroom, painting the deck with brilliant amber swaths.

My phone buzzed in my cargo shorts on the deck beside my bed. Phoebe's warm body was draped around mine. She rolled aside and stirred as I dug the phone from my pocket and swiped the screen.

Denise's sweet voice filtered into my ear. "Hey, I didn't wake you up, did I?"

My voice scratched, "No. Whatever gave you that idea?"

"I know JD had a show last night, and you guys are always pretty wrecked the day after a show. Did you have fun?"

"You could say that."

"Is there a hot little number next to you right now?"

"Why? Jealous?"

She hesitated for a moment. "I'm not gonna answer that."

I chuckled. "What's going on?"

"Kinley Collins. She called the station. Said she's a friend of Nina Harlow's. Said she heard about her death on the news and wanted to find out more information. Said she's pretty sure she knows who killed Nina."

That got my attention. "Sounds like somebody we should talk to."

"That's why I'm calling. I'm going to text you her contact information and address."

"Thank you."

"I was able to pull the phone records for Nina Harlow and Sebastian Simonton. I'll sift through them and make a list of recent contacts and see if anything stands out."

"I'll say it again, you're the best."

"Yes, I am," Denise said in singsong before she hung up.

A moment later, a text buzzed through with Kinley Collins's number. I gave her a quick call. It went straight to voicemail, and I left a message identifying myself as a deputy sheriff.

I climbed out of bed and set my phone on the nightstand, then stumbled into the en suite. I took a shower, toweled off, then stepped back into the compartment.

Phoebe had my phone to her ear. She handed it to me. "It's some girl calling for you."

I gave her a quizzical look. "You answered my phone?"

"I thought it might be important. Sorry."

I took the phone from her and held it to my ear. "Hello?"

"Deputy Wild, this is Kinley Collins returning your call."

"Yes, thanks for calling me back. You called the station about Nina Harlow. I'm so sorry for your loss."

"Thank you."

"You mentioned to one of the deputies that you have information we should consider. Do you have a moment to speak today?"

"I'm booked on a photoshoot all day, but you can stop by the set."

"That sounds great. I take it you're a model?"

She seemed amused by the question. "I prefer the term *on-camera personality*."

"*On-camera personality* it is."

"I'll text you the address. Maybe you could show up around lunch?"

"Sounds perfect."

"I'll see you then, Deputy."

She ended the call, and I set the phone back on the nightstand, then moved to the dresser and pulled out a pair of boxers, shorts, and a T-shirt.

"I hope you don't think I was invading your privacy," Phoebe said. "I just heard you on the phone earlier. It sounded like urgent police business."

"Not a problem. Thank you."

I tossed the towel aside, and Phoebe's sleepy eyes perked up. She watched me get dressed, biting her bottom lip with hungry eyes.

"You want breakfast?" I asked.

She nodded. "Yes, Daddy."

I chuckled. "How do you like your eggs?"

"Scrambled."

"Scrambled eggs, coming right up."

I left the stateroom, spiraled downstairs, and made my way to the galley. As usual, the place was a wreck. There were empty beer bottles and glasses everywhere. I peered into the salon, and there were people crashed on the settee, the sofa, and on the deck. It was too early for most people to even consider waking after a night like that.

I put on a pot of coffee, sizzled bacon in a pan, and whipped up some scrambled eggs. I was surprised that the aroma didn't draw the party zombies.

I dished up two plates and carried them on a tray with orange juice and coffee up to my stateroom.

Phoebe had fallen back asleep and had pulled the pillow over her head.

"Wake up, sleepyhead," I said.

She pulled the pillow aside and peeled her eyes open. "That's pretty impressive. I didn't even put out, and I'm still getting breakfast in bed."

"I'm a generous guy. What can I say?"

She smiled. "I can only imagine what will happen when you finally put it inside me."

I swallowed hard. The captain definitely perked up on that statement.

15

I took Buddy for a walk. It was a beautiful morning—clear blue sky, cool breeze, amber rays glistening across the water. This truly was paradise.

When I returned to the *Avventura*, I banged on the hatch to JD's VIP stateroom, trying to roust him out of bed. The day was quickly evaporating, and we had a lot to accomplish.

I had searched the Internet on my phone, hoping to learn more about Kinley Collins. She was definitely someone Jack would want to meet.

A groan emanated from the stateroom, indicating JD was still alive.

I banged on the door again.

"I'm up," he grunted.

He fumbled around inside the compartment for a minute, then pulled open the hatch, looking like he'd been hit by a Mack truck. His hair was tousled, and his eyes were puffy and red.

I chuckled. "Have a good time last night?"

With a mischievous grin, he nodded to the queen berth. Two naked hotties stirred, and that was all the answer I needed.

Jack stumbled out of the VIP stateroom and listed toward the galley. His face crinkled upon arrival. "Where's breakfast?"

"You missed it."

He shot me a sour look, then pulled open the refrigerator and surveyed the contents. His frown deepened. "We're out of eggs! And there's only a squirt of orange juice left."

"We're out of a lot of things."

He closed the door, pulled open the freezer, and grabbed the last breakfast taco. He peeled it from the wrapper, put it on a plate, and stuffed it into the microwave.

"There was a full gallon of orange juice in there last night," he said.

"I guess somebody likes screwdrivers."

The bell dinged, and JD pulled the breakfast taco from the microwave. He gobbled it down, then stumbled back to his stateroom and took a shower. When he emerged, he had a little more life in his eyes.

Signs of life were beginning to appear as the drunken revelers stirred. We rousted the strangers and sent them on their way. There were plenty of nooks and crannies aboard the boat for a drunk to crawl into and pass out during the night. It was a cruel morning for many.

By this point in time, the guys in the band had each staked a claim to the below deck guest rooms. We left them undisturbed.

Phoebe had gone back to sleep after breakfast, trying to steal a few extra minutes of shut-eye. I kissed her on the cheek and told her to lock up if she was the last one to leave the boat. I had her number in my phone and told her I would call her later.

She gave a sleepy response and pulled the pillow back over her head.

JD and I left the boat and ambled down the dock to the parking lot.

"Don't forget, we told Teagan we'd take her to the range today," JD said. "Though I'm not particularly in the mood for loud noises right now."

I laughed. He looked like his head was still pounding. "I'll text her and see if she still wants to go today."

After I tapped out a message to Teagan, I showed JD a picture of Kinley Collins on my phone. I had pulled it from the Internet. "This ought to brighten your day."

Jack's eyes perked up as he surveyed the gorgeous blonde. Her svelte body arched in a provocative pose. She wore skimpy lingerie that left little to the imagination. "One of Nina Harlow's friends?"

I nodded.

"She looks suspicious," JD joked. "She may be hiding something. I think she'll require a rigorous interrogation. Possibly a strip search."

We hopped into the Porsche and zipped across the island to the marina at *Pelican Point*. Kinley's photoshoot was aboard a 145' *Valenti* named *Daydreams*. It was the epitome of style and sophistication—elegant windswept lines and graceful curves. The interior styling was created by the famed Italian designer *D'Agostino*.

Camera flashes spilled from the salon as we stood on the dock, marveling at the massive vessel. JD's face scrunched, and he shook his head dismissively. As nice as it was, the boat didn't hold a candle to the *Avventura*. Even if it did, Jack would never admit it. We'd already overspent our boat allowance, and I certainly didn't need him getting any ideas about an *upgrade*.

We crossed the passerelle and stepped to the aft deck. There was a U-shaped settee and an alfresco dining area that offered a panoramic view.

An assistant saw us through the glass and pulled open the sliding salon door. The slender, snooty man barked, "This is a private shoot."

JD rolled his eyes and flashed his VIP pass.

The snooty man's lip curled, and a subtle groan escaped his smug face.

"We've got an appointment with Kinley," I said.

16

K inley posed in front of the camera, her stunning body on full display. And I do mean *full display*. Her sultry pose changed subtly with each flash. Her eyes smoldered into the camera, and her plump lips softly puckered.

Her gaze was electrifying.

Kinley's platinum blonde hair fell to her mid-back, and her lightly tanned skin had no blemishes or imperfections. A makeup artist would dart into frame occasionally to adjust a stray hair or powder her nose—not that she needed it. She was a goddess, casting spells of desire on all who witnessed her beauty.

Kinley had failed to mention that she would be totally nude —which certainly didn't draw any protest from us. We stood on the sidelines, watching the photographer snap photos of the scorching vixen. We tried to keep our tongues in our mouths. Kinley could certainly perk you up better than any cup of coffee. She arched her body for the lens, accentuating her glorious curves.

I could see the wheels turning in JD's mind.

After a few minutes, the photographer shouted, "Okay. Take five while I review the images."

He handed the camera to the snooty assistant, who popped out the flashcard and downloaded it onto a laptop.

The makeup artist rushed to Kinley and helped her put on a luxurious robe. She tied it at the waist and sauntered toward us. Kinley extended her hand, and we shook. "Deputy Wild?"

"Yes. And this is Deputy Jack Donovan."

"Thanks for coming. I'm so devastated about Nina. She was my best friend."

We offered our condolences, and Kinley led us forward to a guest stateroom that she had been using as a dressing area. Inside the compartment, there was a clothes rack with an array of bikinis and lingerie items, though they didn't seem to be getting much use.

"Is this your boat?"

"No, I'm renting it for the day."

"What is the shoot for?" JD asked.

"My personal website," Kinley said. "I'm always doing photo-shoots to create new content for subscribers."

"I would imagine you have a lot of subscribers," JD said.

A slight smirk tugged at her full lips. "I do. And I like to keep them happy. At last count I had 9,633. At $4.99 a month, it's not a bad living. I'm going to do something special when I get to 10,000."

"That's impressive," I said.

"I have over 1 million followers on *Instabook*. My social media presence basically funnels them into my private website."

"You know, we have a very nice boat that I think you might be interested in for photoshoots," JD said. "Much nicer than this."

Kinley arched a curious eyebrow. "Really? What is your location fee?"

"We could offer you a package deal," JD said. "Tyson and I are both photographers."

Her eyes narrowed with skepticism. "Real photographers? Or *guys with cameras,* looking to fill their spank banks?"

JD smiled. "Do either of us look like we need a spank bank?"

Kinley's eyes flicked between the two of us. She looked me up and down. "Well, he certainly doesn't."

JD frowned at her.

I tried to stifle a grin. "You mentioned you may have a lead about Nina's death," I said, trying to steer the conversation back on track.

It was hard to concentrate on anything but Kinley, especially with the way the robe was falling open and failing to cover her pert bosom. I'm sure she was used to the gravitational pull of her assets.

"Shane Brown," Kinley said. "That's who you need to be looking at. He killed her. I know it."

"Who is Shane Brown?" I asked.

"Nina's ex-boyfriend. I knew he was bad news from the moment they met. I warned her, but she wouldn't listen. They dated off and on for about a year, and it was always tumultuous. He was verbally and physically abusive with her. They'd break up, then he'd pull her back in. He's a classic narcissist, and I just don't understand how Nina couldn't see through his BS. He'd *love bomb* her, tell her she was the greatest thing in the world, profess his undying love, then he'd turn manipulative and berate her. He tried to separate her from family and friends. Classic stuff. He tried to create a wedge between us. He lied to Nina and told her that I came on to him." Her face twisted in disgust. "Sorry, but I wouldn't screw him if he was the last man on the planet."

Kinley certainly wasn't hurting for options.

"What was the current status of their relationship?" I asked.

"She had broken up with him a year ago. He flipped out and harassed her incessantly. She got a restraining order against him, and I think it just recently expired a few months ago."

"Do you know if Nina had been in contact with Shane recently?"

Kinley sighed. "I don't know. She didn't say anything. But she might not have wanted to upset me. She knew how I felt about that guy."

"I take it that you were able to convince her that you didn't hook up with Shane?"

"Yes. And it was pretty obvious to her when she actually thought about it and was able to break free of his spell."

"What about Sebastian Simonton?" I asked.

17

"I liked Sebastian," Kinley said. "I thought they were good together. He was a little younger than she was, and I don't think he was looking for anything serious, but they were having fun."

"You think Shane followed them out to *Eel Reef*, boarded their boat, and shot both of them in a jealous rage?" I asked.

"That's exactly what I think happened. I mean, it's pretty obvious to me."

"And how was your current relationship with Nina?"

Her pretty face crinkled. "What do you mean?"

"Were you getting along?"

"Yes. I told you we were besties. We'd put all that nonsense behind us. We were like sisters." Her eyes misted. She wiped them delicately so as not to smear her mascara.

"Did Nina ever talk to you about her clients?"

"Never any details. Patient confidentiality, that kind of thing. But sometimes she would talk in general terms."

"Did she ever mention anything concerning?" I asked. "Perhaps an infatuated client? She *was* a beautiful woman."

"She was definitely a heartbreaker," Kinley said.

"Did she ever mention anyone in particular?" I pressed.

Kinley hesitated. "Well, I guess it doesn't matter now. It's not like she's going to get in trouble." She took a deep breath. "Nina told me that she had a client that was scaring her. He became fixated and got upset when she declined his advances. She had to stop treating him and referred him to another therapist."

"How upset?"

"She didn't go into details. She just mentioned it frightened her."

"Who did she refer him to?"

"A colleague of hers. Lillian Hughes. I like her. She's spunky and has a really great, dry sense of humor."

"You know the name of this client?" I asked.

"No. She wouldn't tell me."

"Do you know if this client ever made threats or assaulted her physically?"

"Again, she didn't go into specifics. But I think he showed up at her boat a few times. She may have called you guys on him, now that I think about it."

I exchanged a glance with JD. We could look up the records and see if Nina had made any complaints.

"What time frame was this happening?" I asked.

"I think this was about three or four months ago. She hadn't mentioned it lately, so I assumed that the harassment just went away. Honestly, I didn't think of it until I started talking to you."

"Nina had a pretty large merchandising empire," I said. "Was she doing that by herself? Surely she had business partners."

Kinley made a face. "Lloyd." She rolled her eyes. "We both knew Lloyd from the adult film days. He gave us our first break in the business. Don't get me wrong, Lloyd is... well, *Lloyd*. Kind of a sleaze-ball. I'm not really sure why she partnered with him, other than the fact that he does have a lot of connections in the industry. He was able to get the novelty items up and running quickly with very minimal effort on Nina's part. She didn't really want to deal with that side of it, but it was a no-brainer to sell the merchandise as her popularity grew."

Do you have contact information for Lloyd?"

"I do. I can send it to you if you'd like."

"Please. And Lillian Hughes, if you have it."

She grabbed her phone, and her nimble fingers shared the contact information. My phone buzzed with a text from her a moment later.

"Do you think Lloyd would have any incentive to kill Nina?" I asked.

Kinley thought about it for a second. "I don't think so. Nina was the face of the brand. I would imagine her death is only hurting sales."

"Can you tell me where you were Wednesday evening?"

She tucked her chin and lifted an eyebrow, clearly offended. "You're asking me where I was?"

"Just being thorough, ma'am."

"I was online, camming with my fans. There were 3,000 guys in an online chat room, watching me do naughty things. I can assure you, I had no involvement in Nina's death." She paused. "If you want proof, you can become a subscriber to my website and get access to my archives of online videos and cam sessions, which are time-stamped."

Kinley was an entrepreneur. No doubt about it.

18

T he makeup artist banged on the hatch and called into the compartment. "Kinley... Peter is ready for you."

"I'll be out in just a minute," she said. Kinley smiled at us. "Duty calls."

"Do you know where we can find Shane?" I asked.

"That loser bartends at *Blackbeards*."

I gave her my card and asked her to contact me if she could think of anything else. I could tell JD wanted to hang around and watch the rest of the shoot, but we had business to take care of.

Teagan finally texted me back. *[Yes, we are still on.]*

[What time?]

[Whatever works for you guys?]

I consulted with JD.

"Let's do it now, then grab lunch," he said. "We can follow up on these leads in the afternoon."

I texted Teagan back, and I told her to meet us at *Bull's-Eye* in 20 minutes.

She replied: *[Great, I'll reserve a lane.]*

We left *Daydreams* just as Kinley disrobed in front of the camera. JD nearly tripped over himself, craning his neck to look as we stumbled out of the salon.

We crossed the aft deck and traversed the passerelle to the dock. I called Denise and asked her to get information on Shane Brown, as well as any complaints from Nina Harlow over the last 6 months.

We hopped into the Porsche and cruised across the island to the indoor range. *Bull's-Eye* was the premier firearms facility on the island. It offered 24 state-of-the-art indoor lanes. There was a live-action virtual simulator, an on-site gunsmith, gun rentals, a retail store, and a VIP lounge. It was an oasis for gun owners. You could rent lanes by the hour or purchase monthly subscriptions. All first-time firearms users were required to take an on-site safety course which covered basic operation, safety, and loading and unloading procedures. Teagan had already completed the basic course days earlier. She waited for us in the retail area.

The muffled sounds of the firing lanes were barely audible through the soundproofing. There were T-shirts, holsters, ammunition, and a host of other gun-related accessories for sale.

Teagan greeted us with a wide smile. "You guys ready to do this?"

"You know it," JD said.

We donned our eye and ear protection and spoke with the range safety officer. Steel and aluminum cased rounds were prohibited. Only brass and nickel were allowed. Our ammunition was thoroughly inspected by the safety officer before entering the range. We had to fill out *assumption of risk* forms and *indemnity waivers*. Once all the *I's* were dotted and the *T's* crossed, the range safety officer gave us the clear to enter.

Bull's-Eye was a continuous live-fire range, and shooting would only be stopped for emergencies. There were cameras on every lane. If shooters needed assistance, all they had to do was wave. If they broke a rule, the safety officer would be on top of it quickly.

There were no hand-to-hand transfers allowed and no lane-to-lane transfers. Weapons had to be placed on the bench.

Teagan placed her gun case on the bench, unzipped it, pulled out the weapon, and placed it on the bench as instructed.

I clipped on a zombie target and sent it downrange 15 feet. Most handgun battles occur within confined quarters at short ranges—even then, the hit percentage is small.

I gave Teagan pointers on stance, grip, aiming, and trigger discipline. I told her to aim center mass and to double tap for good measure. The recoil would lift the barrel slightly, putting one round into the chest and another into the head.

If you're going to shoot. Shoot to kill.

Teagan took aim, held her breath, and squeezed the trigger twice.

Muzzle flash flickered from the barrel, and the report echoed amidst the cacophony of sound. The sharp smell of gunpowder filled the lane, and smoke wafted from the barrel.

I looked downrange to the target—she had put one round dead center in the chest and another right between the eyes.

I chuckled. "I don't think you need lessons. You're a natural."

Teagan smiled and took aim again. She squeezed the trigger twice again, repeating her performance. She was dead solid perfect. It wasn't a fluke.

19

W e went through several boxes of ammunition, and I was pretty sure Teagan's hand would be sore in the morning. It didn't matter—she had a beaming smile on her face as we left *Bull's-Eye*.

"I gotta say, I'm impressed," JD said.

"I owe it all to my instructors," she said graciously. "I just hope I never have to use it."

"Better to be prepared," JD said.

"I certainly wouldn't want to be on the business end of that pistol of yours," I added.

We hopped into the Porsche, and Teagan followed us to *Eddie's Grill*.

Denise had called and left a voicemail while we were at the range. She followed it up with a text. *[Looks like Nina called the department a few months ago to make a trespassing complaint against a guy named Royce Lane. She ultimately declined to press charges. Might be someone to look at.]*

I texted back. [Thank you. Anything on Shane Brown?]

[Just the expired restraining order, an assault charge, and a misdemeanor trespassing charge.]

[He assaulted Nina?]

[No. Bar fight. Case was dismissed.]

She sent another text with Royce's information. I was a little surprised by his address.

Eddie's was a little hole in the wall in a strip center. At first glance, you wouldn't expect much from the place, but Eddie cooked a damn good burger. He was quite entertaining about it, too, flipping patties in the air, tossing slices of cheese atop them like he was dealing cards. The grill was behind the bar counter in plain view of the customers.

It was a small mom-and-pop operation, and Eddie's wife ran the register. It had that old-school diner vibe. There was a jukebox in the corner and vintage memorabilia on the walls. There were pictures of big convertible Cadillacs with flared wings and tail lights that looked like rockets. There were road signs from across the country, as well as license plates and old gas station logos.

Eddie had immigrated from Russia and loved classic Americana. His personal Daphne Blue '57 Chevy was parked out front. Eddie's real name was Vladimir, but he didn't think *Vladimir's Grill* would be a good name for a burger joint.

Eddie had a thick Russian accent, and he loved to crack one liners as he hovered over the grill. If you caught him between the lunch and dinner rush, he'd tell you stories about the old days in the former Soviet Union. He had a hard face and a nose that looked like it had been hit with a cast iron skillet more than once. He was a stocky guy and stood about 6'2". From some of the stories he told, I gathered he had intelligence experience. One thing was for certain—he loved America, and he loved freedom.

Teagan celebrated her newfound skills by indulging in a greasy cheeseburger and washing it down with a rootbeer float. Not like it would have any effect on her flat waistline.

After lunch, I gave Teagan a hug and congratulated her again.

"So, when are we doing that again?" she asked. "I think I'm addicted."

"You're welcome to go anytime we do," I said. "It's a perishable skill, and you need to stay on top of it."

She smiled and hugged me one last time before saying goodbye. And I didn't mind the hug at all.

We left *Eddie's* and drove to Shane Brown's apartment on the northeast side of the island. Denise had texted me the address. JD parked in the visitors' lot, and we gained access to the lobby. We took the elevator to the third floor and banged on apartment #312.

A few minutes later, a groggy voice shouted through the door. "Who is it?"

"Coconut County," JD said. "We'd like to ask you a few questions."

The peephole flickered as Shane peered through it. An instant later, the deadbolt unlatched, and Shane pulled the door open. It was midday, but as a bartender, Shane wasn't an early riser. I had hoped we'd catch him off-guard, and it looked like we did.

Shane had strong features—a square jaw, blue eyes, and brown hair that was a little shaggy and tousled. He was 6'1", had an athletic build, and was in his late 30s. He seemed like he did okay with the ladies, and there was certainly something about him that Nina found compelling.

"Is this about Nina?" he asked.

"Yes," I said. "Do you mind if we come inside and chat?"

"Uh, yeah, sure. I guess," he said, then stepped aside.

We entered the apartment and walked down the foyer into the living room. It was a studio apartment, and Shane slept on a futon that was unfolded, taking up most of the small room. The bedsheets were rumpled, and a dying fern in the corner with shriveled, brown leaves attempted to give the place life.

In front of the futon were a flatscreen display and entertainment system. The small kitchen was messy, with dishes piling up in the sink. There were a few empty beer bottles lingering around, and the place smelled like dirty clothes. The balcony opened to a stunning view of the... neighboring apartment complex.

Perhaps Nina thought of Shane as a fixer-upper. He was a far cry from a wealthy guy like Sebastian Simonton.

"You guys have any leads?" Shane asked.

"A few," I said.

"I'm just devastated," he said. "I heard about Nina's death on the news, and I just lost it. I started shaking. I couldn't finish work last night. I had to get somebody to cover my shift. I came home and probably had too much to drink."

JD and I exchanged a glance. He seemed genuinely shaken by Nina's passing.

"When was the last time you saw Nina?" I asked.

"A week ago Sunday."

I lifted a curious eyebrow. "Where at?"

"We went out for sushi at *Blowfish,* then went back to her boat."

I stared at him, surprised. "So, you went on a date with Nina?"

"Yeah. We'd gone on a couple recently."

"Really?"

"We were sort of on the path to getting back together. At least, that's where I hoped it was heading."

"How did that come about? I thought you weren't her favorite person."

"We had our difficulties in the past. But I've done a lot of work on myself. I made some changes. I apologized for the mistakes I made. Fate brought us together. We happened to bump into each other one night about a month ago at *Keys* and just reconnected. It was like magic. All the past evaporated, and that spark was there again. I ended up going home with her that night."

"Did anyone else know about your relationship?"

"I don't know. I didn't tell anyone. I didn't want to jump the gun. I didn't really know where it was going. My friends would think I was crazy if I said we were back together."

"Did you know that Nina was seeing Sebastian Simonton?" I asked.

Shane frowned. "No. I didn't. Not until I saw it on the news."

"How'd that make you feel?"

His face tightened. "How do you think it made me feel? What are you, my fucking therapist now?"

20

"Where were you Wednesday evening?" I asked.

Shane's face twisted into a scowl. "I was working. You don't seriously think I had something to do with this?"

"Well, you did have a tumultuous history with Nina," I said.

His jaw clenched. "I told you, we worked through our differences, and we were making progress. We had a real connection—the kind you only find once-in-a-lifetime. Nina had just given me a second chance. No way was I gonna screw that up."

"Even if you saw her with another man?"

His face reddened, and the veins in his neck swelled. "That's something I don't want to think about, but thanks for the visual."

"So, the idea of Nina with Sebastian made you mad?"

"When I heard she was with him at the time of her death, I was both angry and hurt."

I paused. "You own a boat?"

"Yeah, why?"

"Nina was killed on the water near *Eel Reef*."

"And what, you think I followed her out there, snuck aboard her boat like some kind of Navy SEAL, and assassinated her and Sebastian?"

"It's something to consider," I said.

He scoffed. "That's ridiculous. Check with the bar. I was working that night. And I haven't had my boat out of the marina in over a month. It's got a slight engine problem, and I don't have the funds to fix it right now."

"What marina?"

"Salt Point Harbor."

"What type of boat?"

"A little 25-footer. Nothing special, but it gets me around. Or, at least, it used to."

"Does it have a name?" I asked.

He hesitated.

"I can check the registration and find out."

"*Nina*."

JD and I exchanged a subtle glance.

"I know. It's a little much, but she was everything to me. I wanted to honor her."

"Do you own a gun?" I asked.

His brow crinkled dismissively. "No. I'm not a violent person."

"Except for the assault charge," I muttered.

His eyes narrowed at me. "That was a stupid fight in a bar that I didn't start."

We stared at him for a long moment.

"I don't like where this is going. I think it's time you gentlemen leave."

"We'll be in touch," I said in a slightly ominous tone before leaving the apartment.

We ambled down the hallway to the elevator. JD pressed the call button. "I'd say he's a little obsessed."

"What gave it away?" I asked with a healthy dose of sarcasm.

"The eyes, man. It's in the eyes."

We took the elevator down to the lobby and hustled out of the building to the Porsche. I figured we'd pay Royce Lane a visit, then check out Shane's alibi at *Blackbeard's*.

We headed across town and rolled through the posh neighborhood of *Stingray Bay*. The lawns were green, the hedgerows trimmed, and there were plenty of palm trees towering overhead. All the McMansions shared similar design elements, and they each backed up to a canal that was home to luxury watercraft. It must have been in the HOA bylaws that every resident had to own a black or white sport utility vehicle. They lined the driveways along with Bentleys, Porsches, Mercedes, and BMWs. It was the kind of neighborhood where you had to keep up with the Joneses—and the Joneses were pretty well off.

We pulled to the curb at 1216 Mako Way. We hopped out, marched up the walkway, and rang the video doorbell. JD held his badge in front of the lens.

A nervous voice answered. "Can I help you?"

"Royce Lane?" JD asked.

"Yeah."

"We'd like to talk to you for a moment about Nina Harlow."

He hesitated. "It's so devastating," he broke down into sobs before completing the sentence.

There was a long pause as static crackled over the intercom.

Royce sniffled and pulled himself together. "I'm sorry. I'm just having a really hard time with it. That's all."

"Can you come to the door?" I asked.

"Certainly."

The light on the video doorbell went off. A few moments later, through the frosted glass of the front door, I saw Royce's figure approach. He pulled open the door, wiping his eyes as he stepped aside. "Please, come inside."

We walked into the foyer, onto the Italian marble. An ornate staircase spiraled up to the second floor. There was a parlor to the left and a dining area to the right that connected to the kitchen. Straight ahead was the living area. It had high vaulted ceilings and large windows that offered a view of the canal and Royce's yacht.

The place was decorated with modern leather furniture and expensive art on the walls. I noticed a large portrait that had an uncanny resemblance to Nina.

A glass coffee table was surrounded by a sofa and a pair of chairs. There was a large digital fireplace. You didn't need a real one in Coconut Key.

Royce offered us a seat. "Can I get you anything to drink? Bottled water? Coffee?"

"No thank you," I said.

I noticed a picture in a silver frame on the coffee table of Royce and Nina, arm in arm. I picked up the frame and examined it.

Royce noticed. He looked uncomfortable.

"When was this taken?" I asked, facing the picture toward him, though he already knew what the picture was.

He squirmed. "Actually, that's not exactly real."

I lifted a curious eyebrow.

"I photoshopped images of us together."

"Why?"

Royce was not a particularly attractive guy. He had a round face and thinning straight black hair. He was a little thick around the midsection but not overly so. He was maybe 5'6" with shoes on. The mid-30s geeky guy had brown eyes and wore thick glasses. The magnification bulged his eyes like an insect's.

"I don't know," Royce said. "The power of positive visualization."

As I looked about the living room, there were multiple photographs of Royce and Nina. "Are these all fake images?"

His head tilted, and his eyes narrowed at me. "I wouldn't call them fake. They're just not real."

"I see," I said dryly. "What do you do for a living, Royce?"

"I'm a software developer."

"What kind of software?"

"Mobile apps," he said. "I offered to develop an app for Nina, but she declined."

"You work from home?"

He nodded.

"Looks like you do pretty well."

He nodded again.

"Seems like Nina was very important to you."

His eyes brightened for an instant, then he slumped. "Yeah," he said in a heavy sigh. "She was *the one*."

"She was your therapist."

"She was the only person I felt like I could talk to."

"That's because you paid her to listen."

He shook his head. "No. It was much more than that. We had this connection. She just wouldn't allow herself to acknowledge it. I knew she felt the same way."

I exchanged a glance with JD. At this point, we were thinking Royce was a little off his rocker.

"I told her she could discontinue seeing me as a client, but she said something about that being illegal."

"It's a felony to discharge a patient strictly for the purpose of sexual activity."

He slumped even further. "It wasn't sexual. I mean, I'm not going to lie... I wanted that with her. But this was much more. It was spiritual. I thought maybe if enough time went by, we might be able to interact with each other as equals."

"Did you know she was dating Sebastian Simonton?" I asked.

His face tensed. "Yes, and he was no good for her. I know Sebastian, and believe me, he was just using her. He didn't care about her. Not like I did."

That piqued my curiosity. "So, you knew Sebastian personally?"

He nodded.

"How?"

Royce shrugged. "We met at a programming convention. He asked me to work on his project, *Soulmate*. I did a little work on it, and the asshole stole my code."

I exchanged another glance with JD. That was starting to sound like a motive.

21

"That must have made you pretty mad," I said.

"Sure," Royce said. "But I'm going to take half of that company. Just you watch. I've got a lawsuit pending, and I have email transactions, voicemails, and other evidence. Plus, I'm a little obsessive when it comes to documentation. So I can provide ample evidence of what lines of code are mine."

"How does Sebastian's death affect your lawsuit?"

He shrugged. "I don't know. He certainly won't be able to testify on his behalf, will he?"

"That seems like a benefit for you."

"It does."

"Reason enough to murder someone?"

His face tensed. "No. That's ridiculous. I would never do anything to harm Nina."

"Where were you Wednesday evening?"

"I was here, eating pizza and playing video games."

"By yourself?"

"Yes. I don't have a lot of friends in the real world. But I was gaming online with a user named *Crusher667*. It wouldn't be too hard to figure out his IP and track him down."

"What were you playing?"

"*Annihilator 2* in death-match mode."

"What's that?"

"It's a sci-fi game where you have different arenas, and you try to kill your opponent. And don't give me that *violent video game* nonsense. Just because I like to play first-person shooters doesn't mean I'm a crazed maniac."

"Do you own a gun?"

"No."

"What about the trespassing charge?"

He groaned. "That was a poor decision on my part. I'll admit it. Sometimes I can get a little... obsessive." He paused. "I'm hyper-focused on what I do—whether it's writing code, playing a video game, or pursuing an interest. Perhaps I took that a little too far? Regardless, the charges were dropped."

"It's my understanding that Nina referred you to another therapist. Are you currently seeing Lillian Hughes?"

"I don't see how my medical history is any of your business."

"What brought you to see Nina in the first place?" I asked.

"Again, I don't think it's any of your business." He paused. "Look, I don't have the best social skills in the world. I'm awkward with social interactions. Especially with women."

His statement was more than obvious. JD and I exchanged a subtle glance.

"I thought Nina might help me overcome my shyness and could teach me how to become more appealing to women. I don't have a lot of experience with certain things if you know what I mean."

I knew what he meant. "So, you've never been intimate with a woman?"

He nodded shyly. "That's not something I really like to admit."

Royce grabbed a laptop that rested on the sofa beside him. He flipped open the display and started clacking away on the keyboard. "I'll see if I can determine the identity of the user I was playing online games with Wednesday. I'm clearly a person of interest in your eyes, which is, on its face, preposterous."

His hands raced across the keyboard like a virtuoso pianist. His eyes flicked about the screen. Within a few moments, he unmasked the IP address of his gaming partner. "*Crusher667* is most likely Nate Campbell."

"How did you figure that out?" I asked.

"It's amazing what you can find out on the dark web. That's just the name the account is registered to. It could be anyone that has access to that network." His fingers tapped the keys again. "Want the address and phone number?"

I nodded.

Royce told me Nate Campbell was located in New Jersey. I called the phone number Royce had given me, and it went straight to voicemail. I explained the situation and hoped I would hear back.

I texted the IP address to Isabella, my contact at *Cobra Company*. With the clandestine agency's vast resources, she would be able to verify the information Royce had given us. If he was accurate, his speed was impressive. He could certainly have a career in intelligence. Though, it probably wouldn't pay as well as his current endeavors.

Isabella texted me back a few minutes later and confirmed the information Royce had given us.

"Well, if you'll excuse me, gentlemen," Royce said. "I'd like the rest of my Saturday to myself. I'm still mourning."

"Thanks for your cooperation," I said.

We stood up, and Royce escorted us to the door.

"I'm sure we'll be in touch," I said as we stepped outside.

As soon as the door closed, JD said, "That guy's got stalker written all over him. And all those photos. That's a little creepy."

My phone buzzed with a call from Denise as we walked to the car. "I did some digging on Lloyd Chapman. Have you spoken with him yet?"

"No. That's our next stop."

"Well, I've got something you should ask him about."

22

L loyd Chapman's gravelly voice filtered through the speaker in my phone. "Hello?"

"Lloyd, this is Deputy Tyson Wild with Coconut County. I'd like to talk to you about Nina Harlow."

"Sure. It's horrible what happened. I'm still in shock."

"My condolences. Do you have time to meet briefly today?"

"You can stop by the warehouse. I'm here taking care of a few odds and ends."

"You work every Saturday?"

"I'm kind of a workaholic. Plus, it helps to keep my mind occupied. Nina was a dear friend."

He gave us the address to the warehouse before ending the call. JD and I drove across the island and pulled into the parking lot of an industrial row. It was a strip-center of warehouses, each with a loading dock, bay doors, and a small office/reception area. The industrial complex was a relatively new addition—the last 10 years or so. It was the newest part of the warehouse district, several blocks from JD's practice studio.

The parking lot was empty on a Saturday. We pulled in front of the main office. The blackout glass had white lettering that read: *Nina's Novelties.* We climbed the steps, and the door chimed as we pulled it open. There was a small reception area with a desk. A hallway led to a few offices and restrooms. There were a few old chairs in the waiting area and a couple of product posters on the wall featuring Nina proudly displaying erotic items. But this wasn't a place that saw customers. Mostly staff and delivery personnel. Everything was sold online.

I poked my nose down the hallway and shouted, "Lloyd?"

There was no response.

JD and I pushed past the reception desk, making our way down the corridor, beyond the offices and the break room, into the cavernous warehouse space. It was home to rows and rows of novelty items stacked high upon shelves—DVDs, Blu-rays, and unmentionable adult novelty items.

Against a wall, there were full-size, lifelike, silicone sex dolls. They were propped up with stands—their blank, expressionless faces staring into space.

JD's eyes rounded at the voluptuous dolls. At first glance, they looked real. Their hair was inserted into the scalp by hand, one strand at a time, giving a natural look. Their makeup had been applied with silicone paint and looked like something from a fashion magazine—smokey eyes, long lashes, and glossy lips. The eyes were interchangeable and could be ordered in a variety of colors.

JD carefully examined one of the dolls and couldn't resist squeezing her breast—it was fully exposed and begging for attention. The supple silicone conformed to his hand as he kneaded it with curiosity. The boob bounced and jiggled when he let go.

Jack's jaw dropped, astonished. "Feel that! It's almost like the real thing."

"I'll take your word for it."

"Blindfolded, I'd be hard-pressed to tell the difference, except for the temperature."

"They come in all shapes and sizes if you're interested," Lloyd said, emerging from an aisle. He ambled toward us.

Lloyd was 5'8", 200 pounds, balding, with a mustache. He had puffy brown eyes, and he had a slight waddle to his walk. He wore a suit and looked part businessman, part gangster, part used car salesman.

"Everything is customizable," he continued. "We can make them tall, short, curvy, slim. You can have B cups or triple Ds. We can make them trim and athletic or with a lot of junk in the trunk. It's totally your call. You can design your dream girl. Everything works just like it should and feels like the real thing."

"Just out of curiosity, how much?" JD asked.

"Depends on the options. What you're looking at right there is $7,000."

Our jaws went slack.

"$7,000?" JD balked. "Who spends that kind of money on a sex doll?"

"You'd be surprised," Lloyd said. "I can't have the damn things made fast enough. Everything you see here is already sold. For a little extra, they come with a heater, keeping a core temperature at 98.6°. If you want to spend a little more," he said with a smile, "we have a version with sensors in strategic locations, and the dolls will react based on stimulation. You can program their responses to be naughty or nice. It's really state-of-the-art stuff. And the best part, when the romance ends, she doesn't take half the assets." He flashed another sleazy smile, then said in singsong, "I ship discreetly, all over the world."

"What's your bestseller?" JD asked.

"The Nina signature model, of course." He pointed to a doll a few rows down that looked exactly like Nina. It was freaky.

"Everything is anatomically correct on that doll. We actually took molds from Nina's body. If you can't have Nina, that's the next best thing."

"You ever sell one of those to a guy named Royce Lane?" I asked.

Lloyd shrugged. "I can check the sales records."

"What does that mean for business now that Nina's gone?" I asked.

"It's gonna be tough. She was the face of the brand. With her podcast and web show, she was always in the public eye. Let me tell you, that girl sold a lot of lube, condoms, and dildos."

"Speaking of... Nina was assaulted in a way that would indicate a personal connection. Someone with a lot of animosity. Can you think of anyone who wanted to hurt her?"

"Nina was a sweetheart. A really genuine person. You don't see a lot of that today. I think she was doing a good thing, helping couples speak openly and honestly about sex, enhancing intimacy, and creating a meaningful connection." He gave a solemn pause. "There are not too many people I can think of that would want to hurt her, but one comes to mind. I'm sure you talked to that nut job ex-boyfriend of hers, Shane?"

"We did."

"My money's on that guy. He's unstable." Lloyd shook his head. "I don't know what the attraction was."

"Where were you Wednesday evening?" I asked.

He frowned. "I was waiting for you to get around to that. I was here. I'm always here. This is my life. I never really intended to be a purveyor of smut, but life happens."

"Can anyone verify your whereabouts?"

"Yeah. My girlfriend, Ophelia. She brought me dinner and hung out while I finished up some orders. Then we went back to my place."

"I'll need her number."

"Of course," Lloyd said. "But I'll save you some trouble. I didn't kill Nina. She was the golden goose."

"I'm sure with an operation like this, you have insurance?"

His eyes narrowed at me. "I know where you're going with this. Look, this was Nina's brainchild. She incorporated the LLC in her name. She got the insurance policy, and we had a contract between us. I'm sure you boys have done your homework. Because of the past allegations against me, of which I am completely innocent, it's very difficult for me to get insurance. The premiums are exorbitant. For that reason, Nina handled the corporate structure. So, let me be perfectly clear... I stand to gain nothing by Nina's death."

Lloyd had been accused of arson and insurance fraud when a previous warehouse had gone up in flames. It had contained a host of valuables and antique cars.

Lloyd was smart. He had kept his mouth shut, and the case fell apart.

"If Nina was the sole owner of the company, what's the status of it now?" I asked.

"We had a joint bank account with right of survivorship going to me. There was a clause in our operating agreement that the company would pass to me in the event of her death and vice versa. I don't have any kids, neither did she."

"Do you own a gun?"

His face crinkled like it was a ridiculous question. "Hell yes. This isn't the greatest part of town, and sometimes I'm here late with no one around. I don't usually carry a lot of cash around, but some of these punks will kill you over $0.50."

"Can I see the weapon?"

"It's in the drawer in my office. Feel free to take a look."

I nodded to JD, and he shuffled back toward the office.

Lloyd pulled his phone from his pocket and dialed a number. He put it on speakerphone, and a woman answered with a sweet, baby doll voice. "Hey, baby."

Lloyd's gruff tone softened. He'd gone from a pit bull to a poodle. "Hey, doll. Will you speak to this gentleman and tell him where I was Wednesday evening? This is Deputy Wild with Coconut County."

Lloyd handed me the phone.

"Hello, ma'am," I said.

"Is Lloyd in some kind of trouble?"

"No, ma'am. We're just trying to verify his whereabouts Wednesday night."

"Hmm... I brought him dinner around 7-ish. We ate together, and he finished up with a few orders. Then we went back to his place around 9:30 PM."

"Were you with him the entire night?"

"Yes."

"Thank you for your time," I said, then handed the phone back to Lloyd.

"I'll call you later, Doll."

"Love you, Babe."

"I love you, too," Lloyd said in singsong. He ended the call and slipped the phone back into his pocket. The gravelly voice returned. "Satisfied?"

"She's your girlfriend. What else is she going to say?"

Lloyd scoffed and rolled his eyes. "You fucking guys, I tell you."

23

J ack shook his head as he returned from Lloyd's office. ".45 caliber."

"What was Nina shot with?" Lloyd asked, relieved. "A 9mm?"

"Yeah," I said. "I don't suppose you own one."

"No. I'm telling you... you guys are barking up the wrong tree. But I'll sit here and answer whatever questions you have. I ain't got nothing to hide." He smiled.

I filled JD in on Lloyd's alibi.

Lloyd flashed an untouchable smile.

I stared at him for a long moment. "I think that's all for now."

Lloyd escorted us toward the exit. We stepped into the hall-way, heading for the lobby. As we passed his office, Lloyd said, "You mentioned something about an order for one of the Nina signature models. Do you want me to look it up?"

Just to satisfy my curiosity, I said, "Sure."

"What was the customer's name?"

"Royce Lane."

Lloyd took a seat at his desk and typed on the computer. His eyes surveyed the information on the monitor. "Yep. He ordered one last year. All the bells and whistles."

"Thanks," I said.

JD and I continued down the hallway and pushed outside. We hopped into the car and headed back toward the marina at *Diver Down*. The sun angled toward the horizon, and the wind swirled around the cabin as we cruised with the top down. A beautiful array of colors painted the sky.

"Think the girlfriend is covering for him?" JD asked.

"The guy's got a shady past, but I don't think he killed Nina. Not much to gain. He might get a little boost in sales with all the media attention about her death, but in six months to a year, people will have moved on. Sales will dwindle."

"If there's a fire at that warehouse in the near future, we know the reason why," JD muttered.

"Doubtful. He's going to lose his insurance when the company transfers into his name."

"Maybe he'll put the company in his girlfriends name."

I shrugged. Anything was possible.

JD whipped into the parking lot and pulled around by the dock. "What do you say we hit *Tide Pool* tonight?"

"Sounds good to me."

"I'm gonna head back to my house, take a power nap, and get freshened up. I'll call you after a while."

I hopped out of the car and ambled down the dock to the *Avventura*.

Jack dropped the car into gear and peeled out of the parking lot. The engine howled as he launched down the highway.

I was still wrecked from the night before and could use a little shut-eye myself.

Buddy bounced and barked at the salon door as I crossed the passerelle and stepped to the aft deck.

The little Jack Russell wasn't alone.

He had a yappy little friend with him. I instantly recognized the Yorkshire Terrier. It was Cooper.

My face crinkled with confusion. What the hell was he doing here?

I slid open the door to the salon and noticed it was unlocked. I knelt down and petted the two furballs, then pulled the door shut behind me.

The smell of Italian seasonings filled the air, and commotion echoed from the galley. The dogs followed me as I moved through the salon.

Phoebe was at the stove, looking cute. She wore a pair of cutoff jean shorts, and frayed threads dangled around her pert cheeks. A snug tank top displayed her perkiness. A pot of pasta boiled, and there was a jar of marinara sauce on the counter. The remnants of chopped garlic and parsley lingered on a cutting board, and juicy meatballs sizzled in a pan.

"Hey, Babe!" she said with a bright smile.

I knew I didn't have any of the ingredients aboard. Phoebe must have gone grocery shopping.

She dashed from the stove, flung her arms around me, and squeezed me tight. She planted her juicy lips on mine, giving me a passionate kiss. When we broke for air, she said, "I thought I'd fix dinner for you since you were such a good sport last night. I hope you don't mind."

I hesitated. "No. Smells good."

"I brought Cooper to keep Buddy company. They seem to be getting along."

"I'm not sure how Fluffy feels about all this." The aloof white cat was probably plotting against the dogs. "Did you go to the store?"

"Yeah, I picked up a few things after I stopped by my apartment to change and get Cooper. How was your day?"

"Interesting," I said.

"What did you do?"

"Talked to a lot of suspects."

"Ooh, sounds intriguing," she said in a mysterious tone. "I hope you like spaghetti."

"I'm sure it will be wonderful."

"It will be. My meatballs are the bomb."

"I'm sure they are."

"I was thinking after dinner, we could snuggle up and watch a movie."

"Uh," I stammered.

"That is if you don't have other plans. I know you probably weren't expecting me to be here." Her face scrunched up. "It's a little weird, isn't it?"

"I told JD we'd—"

She slumped and frowned before I finished.

"But I can call and cancel," I said. "I mean, who in their right mind would turn down a home-cooked meal from a beautiful woman?"

Phoebe smiled. "On second thought, I should probably go after dinner and let you have your space. We can watch a movie another night." She flashed a coy smile. "I don't wanna be *too* available."

"No. We can watch a movie. Then I'll kick you out," I joked.

"Don't worry. I'm not spending the night tonight. That could be trouble." She had a naughty glint in her eyes.

She moved back to the stove and attended to the meatballs.

"Do I have time to take Buddy for a walk?"

"I already took him and Coop out. You don't have anything to do except relax and enjoy a wonderful meal."

"Sounds reasonable to me." I moved to the fridge and grabbed a cold beer. The top hissed when I twisted it off. I gulped a cold swig.

The spicy aroma smelled divine, and my stomach rumbled with anticipation.

I called JD and told him we'd hit *Tide Pool* another night. He assured me that he would be able to stir up other plans. I took a seat on the settee and relaxed.

My phone buzzed with a call from Nate Campbell. I swiped the screen and held the phone to my ear.

24

"I'm returning a call for Deputy Wild," Nate Campbell said, his voice full of curiosity.

"I'm trying to corroborate a suspect's story," I said. "Were you online Wednesday evening playing *Annihilator 2*?"

"No, that would probably be my son, Mason. What's the problem?"

"Is he available to speak for a moment?"

Nate covered the phone and shouted for Mason. His voice echoed throughout the home. "Mason, there's a police officer that wants to talk to you." There was some commotion on the line, and I heard Nate mutter, "You haven't been doing anything illegal, have you?"

"No," Mason replied.

Nate returned his attention to me. "When you say suspect, you're not talking about some kind of online predator, are you?"

"No, it's nothing like that."

"Hang on a second..."

A moment later, Mason said, "Hello?"

I introduced myself and asked him about the video game on Wednesday night. "Is your screen name *Crusher667*?"

"Yeah." He sounded young, maybe 13 or 14.

"Were you playing *Annihilator 2* with a guy named *Codemaster99*?"

"Yeah, I totally trounced that loser."

I stifled a chuckle. I don't think Royce would be thrilled to find out he had gotten his ass handed to him by a kid. "How long did you play?"

"I got online after dinner, and we played several death matches until maybe 11 PM."

"Thanks," I said. "Put your dad back on the phone."

Mason handed the phone to Nate.

"Mason is not supposed to be up that late, or playing video games for that long, are you?" he scolded. "Is there anything else I can do for you, Deputy?"

"No, I think that's all."

"He's not in any trouble, is he?"

"No," I assured before ending the call.

A disappointed frown tugged my face.

"Is everything okay?" Phoebe asked.

"Yeah. Just a lot of dead ends."

I texted Isabella and asked her to track the GPS data for our suspects' cellphones to see if we could find any discrepancies in their stories. Somebody would have a lot of explaining to do if their mobile was in the vicinity of the murders on Wednesday evening. But I figured, in this day and age, you had to be pretty stupid to leave your phone on while committing a crime.

When the meal was ready, we dished up, and we ate on the sundeck. Phoebe wasn't lying about her meatballs. They were phenomenal. Tender and juicy—a combination of ground pork and beef mixed with breadcrumbs and Parmesan cheese, sautéed and topped with zesty marinara sauce over a bed of pasta. Every bite was a culinary delight. When it was all said and done, I was fat and happy.

We sat on the sundeck, enjoying the cool evening breeze, then took our plates down to the galley. I helped Phoebe cleanup, then we retired to my stateroom and picked out a movie to stream.

Phoebe watched as I put my pistol in the nightstand drawer next to the bed. It was home to a few weapons and extra magazines. I think guns made her a little nervous.

I didn't mind a comfortable night in. Phoebe was gorgeous, sweet, and sexy. Who could complain?

She snuggled beside me, her delicate hand caressing my chest. It didn't take long before she was caressing something else.

So much for an innocent night of watching a movie .

Again, I didn't mind, but I wasn't sure where this was going. I didn't want to get left high and dry. But those fears were put to rest quickly.

Phoebe unbuttoned my shorts to give herself better *access*.

"I figure the least I can do is give you a hand," she said in a breathy voice.

I felt like I was in high school, hoping to get lucky.

Phoebe planted her wet lips on mine, sending a spark down my spine. Our lips collided, and our tongues danced. I peeled off her tank top, and her buoyant orbs bounced free. She wasn't wearing a bra, and her pert nipples had been poking through her shirt all through dinner, taunting me.

Pretty soon, we were both completely naked—our clothes bunched up on the deck and strewn about the bed. Things got steamy, and my heart pounded. Her sweet lips whispered naughty nothings in my ear as she kept demonstrating her skillful hand movements.

Pretty soon, her lips traced their way down my chest, sliding her slick tongue over the ridges in my abs. She teased mercilessly before sliding down to the captain.

Her meatballs may have been good, but her oral prowess was even better.

If this was her idea of *not having sex*, I was okay with it.

25

Rays of morning sun blasted through the windows, filling the compartment. I stirred and wiped the sleep from my eyes. Phoebe's naked body was draped around me.

My phone buzzed on the nightstand with a call from Denise. I snatched it and answered, "Hey, what's up?"

"Good morning."

"Good morning to you."

"I've got some things you may want to follow up on. They're long shots, but..."

"Anything is better than nothing."

"I've been looking through Nina's social media accounts. There's a woman that has been making harassing and threatening comments for a while now."

"Do you think these are valid threats?" I asked.

"I don't know. You know how social media is."

"What is she saying?"

"Basically that Nina was a sinner, and that she should be struck down."

I dismissed the statement. "Anything that could be interpreted as a direct, actionable threat?"

Denise paused as she scrolled through the comments. "Here's one. *One of these days, someone is going to take God's work into their own hands and wipe you from the face of the earth. I hope you choke on the filth that you sell.*"

"That's still vague."

"Given the item you guys found in Nina's mouth, it might be worth talking to this woman."

"What's her name?"

"Eleanor Kensington. I'll text you her contact information and address."

I rolled my eyes. "I know Eleanor."

"Personally?"

"No, but I've spoken with her previously about another case. I seriously doubt she had anything to do with Nina's murder, but I'll pay her a visit. Anything else?"

"There are a lot of comments from a woman named Joan Taylor, who claims Nina slept with her husband. She left a comment on Nina's page. *Looks like you got what you deserved, you harlot.*"

"Again, not exactly a threat."

"Have you talked to Lillian Hughes?"

"Not yet. I left a voicemail, but I haven't heard back."

"I looked over Nina's cell phone records. Over the last month, there were a lot of calls to Sebastian, Kinley, Lillian, and Shane Brown. Both incoming and outgoing."

"Maybe Shane was telling the truth about reconnecting with Nina."

"I don't have the content of their text messages, but there are quite a few of them," Denise said.

"Anything else?"

"That's all I've got for now."

"Good work. Thank you."

"You're quite welcome. I'll talk to you later."

By this time, Phoebe was awake and eyeing me curiously. She tried to sound disinterested when she asked, "Who was that?"

"Denise. She's a colleague."

"Oh. Is she cute?"

"She's terribly ugly," I joked.

Phoebe arched an eyebrow. "She sounded cute."

"You listened to my call?"

"No, but you're right next to me, and your speaker is kind of loud. I couldn't help but catch little snippets." She paused. "I'm sorry. I'm being nosy."

I put the phone back on the nightstand.

"What do you want for breakfast?" Phoebe asked.

"Are you cooking?"

"Of course." She smiled.

"I'll leave it up to your culinary discretion."

Phoebe's smile widened. "What are you doing today? I thought maybe we could go to the beach or take the boat out? Do something outdoors. Enjoy the sun!"

"I can't. I'm in the middle of a case, and I've got some leads to track down."

She made a pouty face. "But it's Sunday. You've gotta take a day off every now and then. Can't it wait?"

"Time is of the essence before this thing slips away. There are two people lying in the morgue right now, and I have an obligation to them to learn the truth and see justice served."

She frowned. "Well, I guess I can let you off the hook for that. I should probably get back to my apartment, anyway. I've already stayed longer than I said I would. I promise I'm not moving in."

"You know what they say... three days is a houseguest, four is a roommate."

She laughed. "I have no intention of being a roommate. Not yet, anyway," she said with a coy wink.

She gave me a kiss on the cheek, climbed out of bed, and sauntered naked across the deck to the en suite.

She looked damn good, the sunlight cascading across her naked body.

Phoebe took a shower, slipped on her clothes from the night before, then made her way below deck to the galley. I pulled myself out of bed and went through my morning routine.

The scent of fresh coffee perked me up as I made my way to the main deck. Phoebe had grilled ham and cheese omelettes, bacon, French toast, and there was orange juice on the table in the breakfast nook. The girl could have been a chef at a five-star restaurant. The food was sumptuous, and the presentation was excellent.

After breakfast, I called JD and updated him on the situation. He said he'd swing by in a bit to pick me up, and we'd talk to Eleanor Kensington and Joan Taylor just to rule them out.

Phoebe and I took the dogs for a walk. When we returned to the boat, I called Lillian Hughes again. This time, she picked up after a few rings. I introduced myself and said, "Sorry to disturb you on a Sunday. I was hoping you had a minute to discuss Nina Harlow."

"Certainly. I'm still a little in shock about the whole thing. I got your message. I've been meaning to return your call. I just wanted to be in the right frame of mind."

"It's my understanding that Nina referred clients to you?"

"Yes, we would refer patients we thought might be a fit."

"How did you two meet?"

"We met during graduate school at Vanden, and we've remained close personal and professional friends since then."

"Are you currently treating Royce Lane?"

"I don't discuss my patients' private medical treatment."

"It's my understanding Royce developed a fixation on Nina, and she referred him to you. He has a pretty solid alibi for the night of the murders. I'm just wondering if he's expressed anything to you that would be concerning."

"As I said, Deputy, it would be counter to the interests of therapy to violate a patient's confidentiality."

"But if a patient has expressed a desire to cause harm, that would require mandatory reporting, yes?"

"If a patient expresses a clear and credible intent to harm, yes, we have a duty to prevent further harm. We do not have any obligation to report clients who confess past crimes. This is often an area of great misunderstanding and conflict. Clients and family members often worry that things they say will be used against them. I assure all of my clients that what they say to me is kept in the strictest confidence. It's something, as therapists, we all hold dear. We can't treat patients who will not open up to us."

"Did Nina ever express any concern to you about any of her clients?"

"She would consult with me from time to time."

"I'm assuming she talked about Royce."

Lillian said nothing.

"Was there anyone else?"

She remained silent.

"Let me phrase that another way. Should we consider any of her clients as suspects?"

"It would be wild speculation on my part to confirm or deny potential suspects in her client base."

It was clear I wasn't going to get any answers from Lillian. "Thanks for your cooperation. If anything springs to mind, please feel free to contact me."

"I will. And good luck, Deputy. Nina was a dear friend."

I ended the call and slipped the phone back into my pocket with frustration. I felt no closer to solving this thing than when we started.

Phoebe was in the galley, cleaning up after breakfast. I started to help her.

"Don't bother," she said. "I've got this. I know it's crazy, but I like tidying up. It's stress relief. I find it soothing."

I laughed. "More power to you. I don't find it soothing at all."

JD called. "I'm in the parking lot. Get your ass out here!"

"I'm on my way." I hung up the phone and told Phoebe, "I gotta run."

"Go. I'll tidy up around here before I leave. Is there anything you want done? Laundry? I could fix lunch or dinner and leave it in the refrigerator for you."

I smiled. "No. I'm fine. But thank you."

She lifted on her tiptoes and gave me a kiss. Her soft lips melted into mine.

"I had fun last night," she said.

"Me too."

"There is plenty more where that came from," she said with a deliciously devious grin.

JD blew the horn, and it reverberated across the marina.

I darted out of the galley and through the salon. I petted Buddy and told him to be a good boy before I left and jogged down the dock. I hopped into the passenger seat and pulled the door shut. JD dropped the car into gear and pulled out of the parking lot as I buckled my safety belt.

"So, how'd it go last night?" he asked, looking for all the juicy details.

26

We found Eleanor Kensington in the cockpit of her sailboat, smoking a cigarette. It was docked at *Mangrove Bay*.

Eleanor was an interesting lady. She was in her mid-60s and had short bottle-blonde hair. Eleanor had certainly been a looker back in her day, and she kept her figure reasonably well—but probably not as well as she would have liked. Over the years, the cigarettes had pickled her face, and her makeup looked like something Picasso might have done. The heavy makeup ended up looking like the dry, cracked flats in Death Valley.

We stepped to the dock by the stern of her boat, and Eleanor smiled, blowing out a cloud of smoke through the side of her mouth. "Deputy Wild, to what do I owe the pleasure?"

"I'm afraid this isn't a social call, Mrs. Kensington."

Her smile faded slightly. "Well, a girl can dream, can't she?"

I flashed a courteous smile. "We'd like to talk to you about Nina Harlow."

Her face soured. "That slut? Thank God she's gone!"

"Well, tell me how you really feel," I muttered sarcastically.

"She shouldn't have been allowed on the airways, spouting that filth."

"So you were a fan of the show?" I said in jest.

"Lord, no! But I did listen on a regular basis just to monitor what kind of depraved things she was saying. For Pete's sake, some things need to remain private. I don't know if you ever listened to her show, but some of the things she talked about were just downright unnatural." Eleanor pointed to the sky. "He sees everything, and let me tell you, everybody gets what's coming to them. Sooner or later."

"So you think Nina deserved to die?"

She raised her hands innocently. Wisps of smoke drifted from the cigarette that was half gone. "I'm not one to judge. I'm just saying..."

"You own a gun, don't you?"

"I sure do."

"A 9mm?"

"I got a 9mm, a .45, a .38 special, and an AR 15 with extra magazines for when the shit really hits the fan."

"You definitely seem prepared. Can you tell me where you were last Wednesday evening?"

"I was right here."

"What were you doing?"

"I had dinner here on the boat with a gentleman caller. We had good conversation, a nice bottle of wine, and enjoyed a wonderful evening," she said with a smile, straightening her posture, lifting her nose with pride.

"And who is this lucky gentleman?"

"It's none of your business."

"We're just trying to verify your whereabouts."

She scoffed. "You don't really believe little old me sailed out on the water at night and crept aboard that whore's boat and shot her, do you? I mean, you two must be getting pretty desperate if you're considering me as a suspect."

"You've clearly expressed a disdain for the deceased," I said.

"It's a free country. I can dislike whoever I want."

"That is certainly your prerogative."

She hesitated, and her face crinkled. "If you must know, his name is Paul. But for God's sake, don't harass the man. He's a fine gentleman. I don't need you two running him off."

"I'll need his contact information."

She gave it to me reluctantly.

"I don't suppose we can see your 9mm?"

She smiled. "Not without a warrant."

"You know I can get the Coast Guard out here, and they don't need a warrant."

She huffed, tilted her head down, and looked over her sunglasses at me. "Call them."

"Mrs. Kensington, this would be a lot easier if you just cooperated."

She stared me down for a long moment. "Fine. But only because you're cute, and I'm innocent."

She disappeared into the cabin and returned a moment later with a small pistol case made of a high-impact polymer. She handed it to me. "It's loaded. Be careful. Try not to shoot yourself."

I knelt down and set the case on the dock, flipped the dual latches, and opened the 11x8" case. A pristine 9mm was embedded in custom-cut foam along with an extra magazine filled with copper rounds.

I pulled on a pair of nitrile gloves, picked up the weapon, pressed the mag release button, and dropped the magazine into my palm. It was loaded with the same ammo as the extra magazine. I slid out a round and examined it. These were 115 grain 9mm full metal jackets. Different from the 124 grain jacketed hollow points used in Nina's murder. The barrel smelled like gun oil, and it didn't appear to have been fired recently. Of course, Eleanor could have cleaned it thoroughly and loaded it with different rounds, but I was reasonably certain that Eleanor wasn't responsible for the murders. I slammed the magazine back into the pistol, placed the pistol in the case, latched it, and handed it back to her. "Thank you."

"Is there anything else?" she asked in a sassy tone.

"I think that's all for now."

"I enjoyed the visit, Deputy. Stop by anytime."

"I would, but Paul might get jealous."

A smile curled her lips. She dug into her purse and lit another cigarette as we strolled down the dock to the parking lot.

"I think she's got a thing for you," JD said with a grin. "Maybe we should invite her to our next party?"

"I don't think she'd like us so much after that."

Denise texted me as we walked across the lot. *[You're going to love this...]*

27

A picture of a buxom blonde centerfold from the late '70s appeared on my phone. The photo Denise sent was desaturated and slightly grainy compared to modern digital images. The girl was damn good looking with a classic hourglass figure and all-natural endowments. The pinup queen wore white go-go boots and nothing else.

JD and I ogled the image.

"I think we might have to invent a time machine," JD muttered, practically drooling.

[Guess who?] Denise texted.

[No way.]

[Yup.]

[You're sure?]

[That's Bebe Doll, a.k.a. Eleanor Kensington. What's the saying? Those who live in glass houses...]

I chuckled and showed the text to JD.

"Well, I'll be damned. Looks like Mrs. Kensington isn't so innocent after all. You know she did some hard partying back in the day."

We hopped into the Porsche and left the marina. I called Paul, and he confirmed Eleanor's alibi. It sounded like he was definitely looking forward to another date with the former pinup queen.

We were hoping to track down Joan Taylor and ask her about her veiled threats on social media. The lead was weak, but Eleanor was right. We were getting pretty desperate for answers.

Sheriff Daniels called with a change of plans. "We have a situation. I need you two to get over to *Guilty Pleasures*, ASAP."

"What's going on?"

"Some nut job is in the store. He shot one person and has his girlfriend and the sales clerk held hostage."

"We are on our way."

I told JD, and he mashed the pedal to the floor. The engine roared, and the acceleration thrust me against the seat as we sped down the road. We twisted through the city and pulled to the curb near *Guilty Pleasures*. It was a few blocks from Oyster Avenue.

Red and blue lights flickered atop patrol cars, and deputies had cordoned off the area. A crowd of onlookers gathered. We hopped out of the car and jogged toward the scene.

Deputy Erickson greeted us, giving us the latest updates on the situation.

Guilty Pleasures was an adult novelty store that sold sexy lingerie and erotic paraphernalia.

"Has anybody talked to the hostage-taker?" I asked.

"We called the store phone a few times. Nobody has picked up. A customer that was in the store managed to escape right as the assailant pulled out a gun. According to her, the perp shot a man and took a woman and the sales clerk hostage."

"Where's the customer that escaped?"

Erickson pointed to a frazzled woman who spoke with Deputy Mendoza. She was early 20s with a petite figure, brown hair, and panicked wide eyes. Her entire body trembled. JD and I approached her and introduced ourselves. She told me her name was Iris.

"Do you know what condition the shooting victim is in?" I asked.

"I don't know. This crazy guy just stormed into the store and started screaming and yelling at this couple that had been browsing through the lingerie. The next thing I knew, he pulled out a gun and shot the man in the belly, then aimed it at the woman. By what he was saying, I gathered she was his girlfriend. As soon as I saw the gun, I ran out the door. He fired another shot, and I heard it smack the glass as I pushed outside. I swear, I could feel the wind from the bullet as it zipped past my head. I'm so totally freaked out right now!"

Erickson gave me the number to the store, and I dialed the line. It rang several times. A shaky, frail female voice answered, "*Guilty Pleasures*, how can I help you?"'

It was an instinctual response.

I identified myself and asked to speak with the assailant. She called to the shooter. "It's the police. They want to speak with you."

"Tell them to back off!"

"He says back off," the clerk relayed.

"What's your name?" I asked.

"Amara."

"Can you tell me if the man that was shot is dead?"

"No."

"Hang up the phone now, or I'll blow your fucking head off!" the angry voice shouted.

The line went dead.

I called back and let it ring... and ring... and ring...

The call went to voicemail.

I dialed again.

Finally, someone answered. The voice on the other end was tense and agitated. "What part of back the fuck off do you not understand?"

"We'll stay back," I said. "Nobody's storming into the store. I just want to talk."

"I don't want to talk. I want you guys to pack up and go away."

"You know we can't do that. You sound upset and scared."

"I'm not scared."

"If you're not scared, you must have balls of steel."

"I do. So don't fuck with me."

"Is it safe to say you're having a bad day?"

"You're goddamn right I'm having a bad day."

"My name is Tyson. What's yours?"

"I'm not telling you my name. Are you crazy?"

I wanted to make a snarky comment, but I thought better of it. *I wasn't the one holding hostages.*

"I have to call you something," I said.

"*Bob.* You can call me *Bob.*"

It clearly wasn't his real name.

"Let me guess, Bob... you caught your girlfriend with another guy buying sexy lingerie. That can only mean one thing, right?"

"She's a little whore, and she deserves to die."

"I bet that's devastating."

"You're damn right it is."

"Does the sales clerk deserve to die, too?"

"I don't give a shit about her."

"If you don't care about her, how about you let her go? A gesture of good faith. That you're willing to negotiate."

"What is there to negotiate?"

"Well, right now, you haven't crossed the threshold."

"What threshold?"

"From what I understand, the man you shot is still alive. The minute he dies, you become a murderer. If you let me help you, maybe we can keep things from spiraling in a direction you don't want to go."

He was silent for a long moment.

"You probably think I'm the bad guy and that I'm trying to screw you over. That I'm trying to pull a fast one on you but I'm not. I'll be honest and fair with you, if you're honest and fair with me. That's not unreasonable, is it?"

He hesitated for a long moment. "No."

"Would it be totally outrageous to send in two paramedics to treat the wounded man and remove him from the store so that you don't get charged with murder?"

There was another unbearable silence.

"No, that's not unreasonable. But how do I know you're not going to send two cops disguised as paramedics?"

"You have my word."

"Who the fuck are you? Why should I trust you?"

"The man you shot needs emergency medical attention. Attention that can only be given by qualified paramedics. I'm not gonna risk that man's life by sending in deputies in disguises and risk more people getting injured. I told you, I'll play fair. We'll work through this without another shot being fired. How does that sound?"

"My girlfriend was screwing that dude. Why should I let you save him?"

"It ain't about him. It's about saving yourself."

28

"I'll allow two paramedics in," the perp said. "That's it. If you guys try anything, I swear it's going to be a bloodbath."

"They're just going to help the victim," I assured.

"No guns. If I see someone with a gun, I'll shoot them on the spot."

"No guns," I assured.

"I'm getting off the phone now."

"I'll call you back when they're about to come in."

He hung up.

We found two paramedics with prior military experience. We rigged them up with small body cameras so we could get eyes and ears into the facility. We also had an extra camera in an equipment case that they could *accidentally* leave behind.

Rotor blades thumped overhead as *Tango One* circled above. The crowd of gawkers on the sidewalks grew larger, and news vans had arrived. Paris Delaney showed up with her crew, and the ambitious blonde began broadcasting.

When the medical team was ready, I called the store. *Bob* picked up the phone.

"They're coming in now," I said. "Let's keep everything nice and easy."

"Okay."

I gave the signal to the paramedics, and they rolled a yellow gurney along the sidewalk. One of them pulled open the door and held it while the other pushed the gurney inside. For the first time, we got eyes on the scene. The cameras wirelessly fed a monitor that we all huddled around.

The hostage-taker looked about 25 years old. He had short brown hair and a slender build. He had his arm around his girlfriend's throat, standing behind her with his pistol to her temple. Her face was contorted with panic, her eyes wide, mascara streaming down her cheeks from tears.

Bob had told the sales clerk to stand in the corner and face the wall. She craned her neck over her shoulder to see the action. Paramedics attended to the gunshot victim and began to stabilize him.

Abdominal wounds can be survivable depending on the extent of the damage, but infection is always a major concern.

The paramedics transferred the victim to the gurney and rolled him out of the store. They pushed him along the side-walk and hurried down the block to an ambulance that was waiting. They loaded him into the back, climbed inside, sealed the doors, and sped away. Sirens chirped, and lights flashed.

"I lived up to my end of the deal," Bob said into the phone. "Now I want something from you?"

"I'll see what I can do?"

"No, fuck that. You *will* do!"

"What do you want?"

He was silent for a long moment. "I need time to think about it."

He hung up.

I texted Isabella and gave her the address of the store, and asked her to see if she could identify the cell phones that were at the location. She texted me back a few minutes later. *[Cell phones are registered to Clarissa Wong, Julie McHenry, and Aiden Arthur.]*

I called the store back in a few minutes. When the perp answered, I asked, "Have you thought about what you want, Aiden?"

"How the fuck do you know my name?"

"You're playing in the big leagues now, Aiden. How about you call it a day? You've already shown good faith, I'm sure the courts will take that into consideration. Don't make it worse for yourself."

"I want an armored vehicle fully gassed up and a speedboat waiting for me at the marina of my choosing."

"Where are you going to go, Aiden? Cuba? Good luck."

"I'll kill everyone in the store right now if you don't meet my demands."

I sighed. "I'll make some phone calls and see what I can do. But it's not like I've got access to what you're asking for."

"This is the big leagues, isn't it? Find a way."

"That's a big ask. I was doing you a favor by taking the victim out of there. How about you do me a favor and send out the clerk? I'll get an armored vehicle on site."

"What about the boat?"

"I told you, I'm not gonna lie to you, and I'm not going to make promises I can't keep. I'll make some phone calls and see if I can come up with a speedboat. But I can't just pull one out of my ass. In the meantime, are you hungry? I can send in a pizza and soft drinks."

"What do you think I am, stupid? I'm not gonna eat anything you send in here. You could fill it with poison or tranquilizers."

"The clerk's name is Clarissa Wong. Send her out, and I'll work on your demands."

"I'm not giving up my leverage."

"She's not leverage. She's just one more hostage you have to manage. Think about it. When you exit the store with the hostages, you gotta get into the vehicle, manage them both, drive to whatever marina you choose, get them both onto the boat, and get out to sea. That's a lot to manage. Have you thought about that?"

He was silent.

"Pretty soon, they're going to have to pee and do other things. They'll get thirsty and hungry. Managing hostages is a real pain in the ass. You're about to figure that out."

He said nothing.

"Tell you what... when you see the armored vehicle pull up, you let Clarissa go. Deal?"

29

Sheriff Daniels arranged for the armored tactical vehicle to arrive as soon as possible. The aggressive beast looked like something out of a sci-fi movie with its giant knobby tires and black angular armored panels. It rumbled onto the scene, the diesel engine roaring. It rolled to a stop in front of the store. The driver hopped out and moved away from the vehicle.

I called Aiden's cell phone. I had gotten the number from Isabella. He seemed a little taken aback when he answered. "How did you get my number?"

"I told you, you're playing in the big leagues now."

Aiden cautiously moved to the window and peered outside, keeping his terrified girlfriend in front of him.

He was right to be cautious. There were snipers with itchy trigger fingers on the rooftops across the street. They were just waiting for the signal.

"I'm a man of my word," I said.

"How do I know there's not a SWAT team in that van ready to pounce the moment I step inside?"

"We can do a video call, and I'll show you the interior of the vehicle. But you need to send out Clarissa first."

He hesitated for a long moment.

"I lived up to my end of the deal," I said.

"Okay," Aiden replied.

We waited anxiously for Clarissa to emerge. A few tense minutes passed before the door pushed open, and the scared sales clerk stepped onto the sidewalk. Her eyes were wide with terror. She sprinted away from the building and ran to the safety of the deputies, where she was evaluated by the EMTs for injuries.

She was immediately debriefed.

"I want to see the inside of the armored vehicle now," Aiden demanded.

I made a face-to-face video call with Aiden and walked to the armored vehicle. I held the phone inside the vehicle and panned the camera around, proving it was empty. There were no SWAT team members inside. But we certainly had a few surprises in store for the perp.

"Satisfied?" I asked.

"I need to think about this," he said before hanging up.

I backed away from the vehicle and re-joined JD, Erickson, Faulkner, and Sheriff Daniels.

"What's the status?" the sheriff asked.

"I don't know," I said. "I think he's getting cold feet. I'm sure he feels safe and secure inside the store. The moment he steps outside, he's vulnerable."

"Well, that little dipshit's in for a rude awakening. If the snipers get a clear shot, they'll take it."

I called Aiden again, but he didn't answer. We all waited on pins and needles for him to emerge.

Then things went south.

A flash filled the store along with a thunderous bang. An instant later, another pop.

The tactical response team swarmed the sidewalk with assault rifles in the firing position. They were decked out in black tactical gear with helmets and bulletproof vests.

We joined them.

An officer pulled open the door, and the team filed inside, clearing the room.

Both Julie and Aiden lay dead on the floor.

Julie had a bullet to her chest, and crimson blood pooled around her body.

Aiden had put the pistol to his head and scrambled the contents of his brain, blasting what little gray matter he had across the racks of white, red, and black lingerie. The frilly garments were stained with chunks of slime.

I deflated, and my throat tightened. I couldn't help but notice boxes of novelty items on the shelves with Nina Harlow's face and signature on the packaging.

I felt hollow.

Brenda examined the bodies, and the forensics team documented the area and collected the evidence. It was all a matter of protocol now.

We wrapped up at the crime scene and headed back to JD's car. Paris and her news crew accosted us along the way, but I wasn't in the mood to talk. "No comment."

"Do you think you could have done anything differently?" she asked.

Maybe she didn't mean it to come off as accusatory as it sounded, but it just hit me the wrong way. I glared at her, seething with anger. My jaw tensed, and I bit my tongue. We hopped in the car and sped away from the curb while the cameras still rolled.

Back at the station, we filled out after-action reports, and Sheriff Daniels assured us we did the best we could. "Keep your chin up, boys. It was beyond your control."

It did little to lift our spirits.

JD and I were more than ready for a drink.

We left the station and headed back to *Diver Down,* cruising across the island in a somber mood. Neither one of us said a word. We pulled into the parking lot and trudged to the bar.

Teagan greeted us with a concerned face. She had two glasses of whiskey waiting. She'd seen the coverage on the news. "Are you guys okay?"

We both gave an unenthusiastic nod.

"At least that sales clerk escaped."

"There is that," JD said.

"Do you know if the perp had a history of violent behavior?" Teagan asked.

I shrugged.

"It's crazy the things people do in the name of love," she said.

"I guess he thought if he couldn't have her, nobody could," JD said.

"That's not love," I said. "That's obsession."

"I think that goes beyond obsession," JD muttered.

We sipped our drinks and commiserated.

"Well, I'm thankful that you two are still alive and in one piece," Teagan said, trying to perk up the mood. She smiled, and I tried my best to smile back.

"I know it's early, but I got cards for you both, and I just wanted to give them to you now." She pulled two rectangular envelopes from beneath the counter and slid them across the bar to us. Our names were written on the envelopes in a girly script surrounded by lots of hearts.

"Should we open these now or wait until Valentine's Day?" I asked.

"Whichever you prefer," Teagan said.

"I feel bad," I said. "I don't have a card for you yet."

An optimistic smirk curled on her beautiful lips. "It's okay. I'm sure you'll give me a beautiful, touching card that expresses your true feelings. And did I mention I like roses?"

I chuckled, then opened the envelope and pulled out the

red card with a giant heart on it. I flipped it open and read a heartfelt note that seemed to encapsulate the dynamic of our friendship. It made me choke up a little. "Aw, that's sweet. I feel the same way about you."

Teagan smiled. She rushed around the bar counter and gave me a hug. The hug lingered, and I didn't mind.

But somebody else certainly did.

Teagan kissed me on the cheek before pulling away.

Phoebe stood in the doorway of *Diver Down* with Buddy and Cooper on leashes. Her eyes narrowed, and her cheeks flushed. The veins in her temples pulsed. "Hey, Babe."

Her tone wasn't friendly.

"Hey," I said, slightly confused by her presence. "I didn't think you'd still be here."

"Obviously." She marched toward me with fire in her eyes. She looked Teagan up and down and practically snarled. "Who's this?"

"This is Teagan," I said, stunned. "She works for me."

"Really?" Phoebe said with an angry arch to her brow.

There was an awkward tension in the room, and Teagan moved around behind the bar and attended to other patrons.

"Where's my hug?" JD asked her.

"You'll get yours later," Teagan said, pouring a draft beer for Harlan, getting as far away from Phoebe as possible. The salty old Marine sat at the end of the bar watching the fireworks. It didn't take a rocket scientist to sense that Phoebe was more than a little jealous.

"Why don't we go for a walk," I suggested, taking Buddy's leash from Phoebe's hand.

JD watched with amusement as we pushed outside.

30

"I thought you were going back to your apartment," I said, the dogs pulling us along.

"Well, I wanted to take the dogs out for one last walk before I left," Phoebe replied. "I spent the day tidying up and doing laundry. Maybe I went a little overboard. Once I start, I just can't stop. It's like a compulsion. I don't mind, though. Like I said, I enjoy cleaning and cooking. It's like therapy."

"You were a little rude to Teagan back there," I said, not mincing words.

She cringed. "I'm sorry, I just freaked out a little bit when I saw her kiss you. I know we don't have anything *formal* going on. It's just a gut reaction. I've had bad experiences with men and infidelity. It triggers me. I hate to use that word."

"Teagan and I are just friends. She's an employee. That's the beginning and end of that relationship. Not that I owe anyone an explanation."

"I understand. Like I said, I may have just gotten a little jealous. That's all. You're not mad, are you?"

"No. I'm not mad. I'm just a little concerned about your expectations."

"Oh, I don't have any expectations."

It certainly seemed like she had expectations.

We walked the dogs in silence for a moment.

"If you want, before I go, I could cook you dinner again?"

"Thank you," I said. "That is a generous offer. It's been a long day, and I think I need a little time to myself to unwind."

She tried not to look disappointed. "Oh, yeah. I totally understand."

We let the fur-balls burn off some energy, then returned to the boat. Phoebe needed to grab her purse and some other items. On her way out, she gave me a hug and a passionate kiss. She broke free and looked at me with her big round eyes. "I know it's probably too soon to say this, but I think you're great. I really enjoy spending time with you. And what we did last night, I don't usually do this soon. And I want to do more." She flashed a naughty smile. "I just don't want to get hurt. I don't know what I'm trying to say other than, I like you."

"I like you, too. I think you're a wonderful girl and a fabulous cook. And we've had a really nice time together."

She smiled.

"But there's no need to rush into anything. We're still getting to know each other."

"What are you looking for? Are you looking for something serious?" she asked, hopeful. "Or just something fun?" She paused and slumped. "I'm sorry, it's too soon for this discussion."

I was feeling a little smothered.

"A little," I said. "But I understand you want to know where this is going. I'm not going to pull any punches. We're both adults. My life is a little complicated right now, and it's difficult for me to prioritize personal relationships. I don't want to hurt your feelings..."

Her eyes filled, and the veins in her temples started to pulse again. She growled, "So, you just want to use me and discard me when you're done?"

Her inner demon surfaced. Her cheeks flushed. I was glad she wasn't holding a sharp object. "I didn't say that."

Her eyes burned into me. "That's exactly what you said."

I paused and took a deep breath. "Okay... I can see you're upset, and I'm sorry if I've offended you." I felt like I was in a hostage negotiation situation again, and I was the hostage. "It's clear we have different expectations and needs. Maybe we should scale things back and maintain a friendship before proceeding any further."

Her eyes rounded, and her lip quivered. Detonation was imminent. "So, you're done with me now? You're just gonna kick me to the curb like trash. You know what, Tyson? You're just like all the rest."

She cocked her arm back and swung with rage. Her open palm smacked my cheek, and the echo reverberated through the salon.

Again, I was stunned.

She knelt down, scooped Cooper from the deck, cradled him in her arms, and marched toward the door. She slid it open, stormed outside, and before slamming it shut, she screamed, "Fuck you, Tyson!"

The bomb had definitely exploded. The glass rattled, and the sliding door hit the frame and bounced back slightly, leaving it ajar.

Phoebe stormed across the aft deck, crossed the passerelle, and marched down the dock. She flipped me off.

I took a deep breath, wondering how that took such a turn so fast. When the smoke cleared, I cautiously made my way to *Diver Down,* hoping not to get ambushed along the path.

JD was still at the bar, and he eyed me with curiosity as I entered. He was just waiting to hear all the details. I took a seat beside him on the barstool.

"She seems a little... *intense*," JD said, putting it mildly.

"You don't know the half of it."

———

31

"I s it safe?" Teagan asked as she tiptoed to our side of the bar. Her cautious eyes surveyed the parking lot for traces of Phoebe. "Where did you find her? That woman is certifiable. How long have you two been dating?"

"That's the thing," I said. "I just met her. She came to the after-party and never left."

"That's what you get for hooking up with random groupies," Teagan said.

"Yeah, you should exercise better judgment," JD said, trying to keep a straight face.

I scowled at him. "You're one to talk. And we didn't hook up. I mean, not totally."

Teagan rolled her eyes.

"I'm serious. We just fooled around a little. But we didn't, you know, seal the deal."

That was met with more skeptical looks.

"I swear!" I said, raising my hands innocently.

Teagan poured another glass of whiskey for me and slid it across the counter. "Man, she got into her car and tore out of here. She almost hit someone as she pulled out."

"I think you dodged a bullet there," JD said. "It's good you got out before it escalated. Might want to run a background check next time."

I rolled my eyes.

"It's like that guy at the lingerie store today," Teagan said. "There are some crazy, obsessed people out there."

Both JD and I deflated.

"Sorry. I shouldn't have brought that up."

JD sipped his drink and patted me on the back. "Well, the night is young. There are plenty of bad decisions ahead. I'm thinking we can find ample at *Tide Pool.*"

Teagan rolled her eyes and attended to other patrons. "You two are incorrigible."

"That's why you like us," JD said.

He looked at his watch. "Let's head over to *Blackbeard's* and see if we can verify Shane's story. Then we can grab dinner at *Wetsuit* and hit *Tide Pool.*"

He'd get no argument from me. I needed a distraction.

We left *Diver Down* and made our way to Oyster Avenue. It was early, and there was plenty of parking on the strip. We strolled the sidewalk to *Blackbeard's* and flashed our badges at the main bar.

I recognized the bartender. He was working the evening of JD's show at *Sonic Temple*. He was a tall, athletic guy with brown hair, thick traps, and bulging biceps. He looked like the kind of guy that could handle obnoxious drunks without much trouble.

"Were you working Wednesday evening?" I asked.

"Yeah, I think so."

"What about Shane Brown?"

"Yeah, Shane was working that night."

"Do you know what time he left?" I asked.

"I think he was here until close."

"You think?"

"As I recall."

"Thanks," I said.

"No problem. Can I get you, gentlemen, anything to drink?"

I gave a glance to JD. He wanted to move on to *Wetsuit*.

"No, thank you," I replied.

A cocktail waitress had stepped to the bar. She had listened in on our conversation. "Shane was here Wednesday, but he cut out early if I remember."

She exchanged a glance at the bartender for confirmation.

"Actually, you're right," the bartender admitted. "Shane did leave early. Sorry, sometimes I get my days mixed up."

"Do you know what time he left?" I asked.

He shook his head. "It's really hard to say."

I gave them my card and took their contact information before leaving. It seemed like Shane Brown's alibi was falling apart.

After we ate at *Wetsuit,* we went to JD's favorite spot. There was a decent crowd at *Tide Pool* for a Sunday night—though, not near the Friday and Saturday night mayhem. It was chill and relaxed with plenty of eye-candy.

We ordered drinks from Harper at the tiki bar, then took a seat at a patio table by the pool and took in the sights. We tried to let the events of the day drift away, but the glum feeling persisted despite the whiskey.

We were halfway through our beverages when JD said, "Uh, oh! don't look now."

"What?"

"Danger, danger," he said in a robotic voice. His eyes flicked across the outdoor pool.

I followed his gaze, looking for the source of concern. "I don't see anything."

JD scanned the patio by the back door. "She was just there a second ago."

"Who? Phoebe?"

JD nodded. "I think she's gone into full-on stalker mode."

I surveyed the patio, but I didn't see any sign of Phoebe. "Are you sure?"

"Maybe I'm seeing things. If it wasn't her, she's got a twin."

"Double trouble," I said.

We stayed at *Tide Pool* for a couple hours, but Phoebe never reappeared. I kept my head on a swivel as we left, pushing through the main bar, exiting the building. We stepped onto the sidewalk, and I scanned the block.

"She's got you a little spooked," JD said with a chuckle.

"You didn't see the look in her eyes when I broke things off."

We made our way back to the car. The whole time I was dreading what we might find. JD's car stuck out like a sore thumb. It was an easy target.

Fortunately, it hadn't been vandalized, and no one was waiting for us. We hopped in, and JD zipped back to *Diver Down*. He dropped me off at the marina and cautioned, "Better lock your doors tonight."

He was thoroughly enjoying this.

I sneered at him.

He dropped the car into gear and peeled out of the parking lot. I headed down the dock, keeping a wary eye, worried that I might be accosted any moment.

32

I had put my phone on *do not disturb* during the night, which is something I rarely do. When I woke up in the morning, there were 147 texts and an almost equal number of voicemails from Phoebe on my phone.

After reading the first few rage-filled texts calling me a *son-of-a-bitch*, among other colorful things, I deleted the thread and blocked her number.

I pulled myself out of bed, went through my morning routine, and fixed breakfast in the galley.

Denise called while I was cooking. "Hey, I found something curious in Knox Murphy's bank records."

"You got a subpoena for the records?"

"Not exactly. But I have my contacts. You're not the only one with resources."

"What did you find out?"

"Knox made a $100,000 cash withdrawal a few weeks ago."

"Is that an unusual transaction for him? The guy *is* a multi-millionaire."

"I'm looking at his transactions over the last year, and there's nothing else of that magnitude. Do you think he could have used that money to hire a hitman to kill Sebastian?"

"It's a possibility to consider. But why? I mean the guy's loaded. How much is enough? And without his partner, the business will suffer."

"You're right. It's probably a stretch."

"It's worth looking into," I said. "Can you do me a favor and do a background check on someone?"

"Sure."

"First name is Phoebe. Early 20s."

"Do you have a last name?"

"I don't," I said sheepishly.

Denise's fingers clacked against the keyboard as she looked up the information. "Phoebe Grant? 24, brunette, blue eyes, 5'3"?"

"That's her."

There was a momentary pause.

"Wow," Denise said, and not in a good way.

"What's her story?"

"She's got a few misdemeanor trespassing charges. An online stalking and harassment charge. There are a few restraining orders against her that are still in effect. There's a destruction of property charge—looks like she keyed someone's car. There are quite a few other things. You want me to list them all?"

My gut twisted. "No. That's enough."

"Who is she? Probable suspect?"

"Not really," I said, cringing.

Denise hesitated. "You didn't bang her, did you?"

"No..." I said, thinly.

"Tyson!?"

"Hang on, you're breaking up. I can't hear you," I said, pretending I had poor reception.

"Tyson, cut the shit."

"It's a long story."

"The girl is troubled."

"I'm beginning to realize that."

"She filed a sexual harassment lawsuit against a former employer, and she made sexual assault allegations against two defendants. One was dismissed, and the other is ongoing. You need to watch yourself."

"I will. Thanks for looking that up."

"Where do you find these people?"

"I'm sorry, there's just no one out there that compares to you, so I have to settle."

She groaned, "Whatever."

"Thanks for the info. I'll talk to you later."

I hung up the phone, and an uneasy sensation twisted in my gut.

I called JD and caught him up to speed. He picked me up half an hour later, and we drove to Knox's mansion in the *Platinum Dunes Estates*. It was a nice home, but not as opulent or as large as I had expected. It looked like all the other McMansions in the neighborhood—although with more exotic sports cars in the driveway. With the recent infusion of cash from the buyout, I'm sure Knox would be upgrading soon.

His wife pulled into the driveway as we arrived. She hopped out of her luxury sport-utility vehicle with personalized plates and carried several upscale bags across the lawn toward the front door.

"Excuse me, Mrs. Murphy," I said, flashing my badge as I jumped out of the Porsche. I advanced up the walkway. "Is your husband home? We have a few questions for him."

"I think you can find him at the country club playing golf."

The girl was a gorgeous blonde with long wavy hair and a slender figure that was decked out in designer attire—black suede knee-high boots, tight black skirt, fitted cream top, oversized Chanel sunglasses with gold accents. A Chanel purse dangled from her shoulder, and lots of diamonds sparkled around her neck, fingers, and ears. Just out of college, Makenna was living the life of a queen.

"Knox recently made a cash withdrawal of $100,000," I said. "Does that seem unusual to you?"

"No, not really."

"That's a lot of money to carry around in cash."

"Not really." She lifted her bags. "I mean, I just spent $72,000 at the mall."

"Impressive," I said.

"If you want to talk finances, you'll need to speak with Knox. I don't have anything to do with that."

"So, he pays all the bills?"

"I have a credit card without a limit." She smiled. "I do whatever I want with it."

"My point, exactly. Most of your purchases are with a credit card. I bet you rarely carry around more than a few hundred."

"So? Maybe he took the cash out to buy me a Valentine's Day surprise and didn't want me to know about it."

"Do you ever look at the credit card bills when they come in?"

"No."

"Then, why bother hiding it?"

She huffed. "Look, I don't know what you're getting at. But Knox didn't kill Sebastian. And he didn't pay anybody to do it either."

"Seems like you know exactly what I'm getting at."

"This conversation is over. Have a nice afternoon, Deputy."

She marched toward the front door, unlocked it, and slipped inside with her expensive bags.

"Guess she told us, didn't she?" JD snarked.

My phone buzzed with another call from Denise. "Hey... Daniels wants you to get over to the *Calliste Apartments*."

"What's going on?"

"You remember that missing person, Emmett Forrester? He's not missing anymore."

33

The atrocious smell wafting through the air curled my nose hairs and twisted my stomach. It could only be one thing. There was nothing else quite like the smell of a rotting corpse.

Erickson and Faulkner had the area cordoned off. There were a few onlookers in the parking garage of the *Calliste Apartments,* gawking with sour faces.

The trunk of Emmett's Lexus was wide open, and flies buzzed about. Inside, Emmett's decaying corpse. Maggots feasted, and the victim's hazy eyes stared blankly into the abyss. There was a puddle of fresh vomit on the concrete nearby.

Cameras flashed as a crime scene photographer snapped photos of the body. Brenda examined the remains. There was bruising on the left cheek like he had taken the punch. At first glance, there weren't any obvious gunshot wounds or punctures.

Emmett's friend, Brody, stood nearby, talking to Deputy Faulkner. I stepped away from the trunk and spoke to him for a minute. His eyes were misty, and he looked traumatized. His face was red, and he was on the verge of losing it. He'd occasionally steal glimpses at the trunk, which soured his stomach and made him gag. The smell was enough to make anyone hurl, which I assumed he did upon discovering the body.

"I kept passing the car on the way to mine," Brody said. "I'm parked two spaces down. I kept smelling something, but I couldn't place it. At first, I thought it was the dumpster," he said, pointing to the beat up green bin just outside the covered parking area. "The smell kept getting stronger. I went up to my apartment, got my spare key to Emmett's car, and popped the trunk. There he was. I tossed my cookies right away."

"Emmett gave you a spare key?" I asked.

"In case he lost his. He was always losing everything."

"How did we miss this?" JD muttered to me.

"I don't know," I grumbled.

I didn't pick up the scent when we previously examined the vehicle. There was a strong breeze that day gusting through the parking garage, and I thought the sour smell emanated from the dumpster.

I walked back to Brenda. She hovered over the body.

"Petechial hemorrhaging around the eyes. There seems to be some indication around the neck that he may have been choked. Judging by the angle of his head, I'd say his neck is broken. I'll know more later."

JD stood beside me, observing the corpse with his face twisted from the stench.

"No wallet, keys, or cell phone," Brenda said.

"He comes home from the bar," I postulated. "Somebody assaults him in the parking lot. There's some kind of scuffle. The assailant punches him, gets him in a headlock, snaps his neck. The perp takes Emmett's keys, wallet, and phone, then stuffs him in the trunk."

"Looks that way," Brenda said.

"Let's go knock on doors and see if any residents remember seeing anything," I said to JD.

After the body was removed and taken to the morgue, we canvassed the building with Erickson and Faulkner. An hour of knocking on doors didn't turn up any leads. Nobody recalled seeing a thing.

The forensics team had dusted the trunk for prints, and hopefully, Brenda could pull the assailant's DNA from the body. Maybe a fiber or other trace evidence might give us a lead.

Jack was hungry, so we headed to *Gators* for lunch. My appetite was somewhat diminished by the ripe body we had found in the trunk. But Jack could easily displace such thoughts. The hostess seated us in a booth by the window and dealt us menus. We perused the offerings and discussed the case.

"Do you think someone was waiting for Emmett in the parking lot? Or did they follow him home from the club?" JD asked.

"Hard to say. We should go back to *Turtles* and ask around again."

"These savages will kill you for a nickel," JD said.

A cute waitress bounced to the table. "Afternoon, gentlemen! I'm Tammy."

Tammy had blonde hair pulled back into a ponytail and brown eyes. Her bangs hung to her brow. She had a cute smile.

"Well, good afternoon to you," JD said, enthralled.

"Are you ready to order, gentlemen?"

"I think we are," JD said.

He ordered the shrimp fettuccine Alfredo. I went with the chicken sandwich. We both ordered diet sodas.

Tammy scribbled our order in her notepad and smiled. "Coming right up!"

She spun around and sauntered to the kitchen to put in our order.

Jack's phone rang. When he held the phone to his ear, an excited voice shrieked through the speaker. I couldn't make out exactly what was said.

"Oh, my God!" Jack mocked. "I can't believe you're actually calling your old man."

It was JD's daughter in Los Angeles. It was a rare occasion, indeed. Scarlett wasn't always the best about keeping in touch. *Life in the fast lane.* She caught him up to speed on the latest happenings. Then he handed the phone to me. "She wants to talk to you."

Scarlett's excited voice filled my ear. "We just started pre-production on *Ultra Mega 2*. I am officially going to be an action movie star!"

"Congratulations!"

"It's crazy. We're having a table read coming up where I'll get to meet the rest of the cast and crew."

"Try not to date your co-star this time."

She huffed and ignored me. "I have my own personal trainer who is putting me through two workouts a day—and let me tell you, they are intense. But I'm going to be buff! I have my own personal nutritionist, and I'm on this crazy diet, and I'm getting a crash course in martial arts training."

"Sounds exciting."

"It is. I don't have a moment to spare. Have you talked to Joel?"

He was our mutual agent.

"No, I haven't."

"The Bree Taylor project is still in post-production, but from what I hear, the studio is really happy with how the edit is coming along, and they're putting even more marketing money behind it."

"That's fantastic."

"And now that I've got a little cash coming in, I think I'm going to look for a new apartment."

"You're moving up in the world."

"I am," she said proudly. "Gotta go. I just wanted to share the good news. You guys need to come see me soon."

"We will," I assured before hanging up the phone and handing it back to Jack.

Tammy returned a moment later and clanked down our entrées on the table.

"Is there anything else I can get you?"

We looked over the meal.

"I think we're good for now," I said.

Sheriff Daniels called as we were about to dig in. I thought about ignoring it, but then thought better of it. I swiped the screen and put the phone to my ear. "I want you guys to get over to the *Platinum Dunes Estates.*"

"We just sat down for lunch?"

"I don't care."

"What is it now?"

34

JD shoveled a heaping scoop of fettuccine into his mouth, puffing his cheeks before digging into his pocket and tossing a wad of cash onto the table. There was no time to finish the meal. We slid out of the booth and rushed out of the restaurant, leaving a confused waitress. We jogged down the sidewalk to the Porsche.

I cringed when I saw Phoebe waiting by the car.

The look on her face was a mix of both sorrow and anger. I felt bad for her. I really did. But she was also starting to freak me out. The first thing I did was look to see if she was holding any weapons.

"I don't understand," she said. "Why won't you talk to me? I've called. I've left messages. You don't respond. Do you just not care anymore?"

"I'm sorry, I don't have time for this discussion right now. We're on our way to a crime scene."

"I know I said a few things in those messages that I shouldn't have, and I'm really sorry. Will you please at least talk to me?"

"I can't right now. We'll discuss this later."

We climbed into the car, and JD cranked up the engine. JD pulled away from the curb, leaving Phoebe looking like a sad puppy dog.

JD cringed. "You're in trouble. The girl has definitely crossed over to the dark side."

"147 texts she sent. And that was before I blocked her."

"Maybe you should unblock her so you can keep tabs on her state of mind. The more intel you have, the better. She's even scaring me, and I didn't bang her."

"I didn't either."

He shot a skeptical gaze in my direction.

"I mean, what was I supposed to do when she put her face in my lap?"

"Well, at least I hope you enjoyed it."

"Dude, it was insane. Seriously. Top 5."

JD contemplated it. "Well, maybe you guys can work things out. I mean, we're all a little crazy."

I frowned at him.

We made our way to 2207 Seascape Drive, not far from Knox Murphy's house. One street over. Deputies Erickson and Faulkner had already arrived, and they were speaking to a woman in her doorway. We parked at the curb, hopped out, and sprinted up the walkway.

The woman was mid-20s with long curly brown hair, olive skin, and brown eyes. Her full lips were even fuller than normal. She had taken a punch to the face that split her lips and puffed them out like she'd been injected with too much lip filler. Her left eye was dark with purple and blue circles. The sclera was filled with blood, and the rest of her cheek was swollen and had a sallow color to it. Tears streaked her mascara. It didn't take a rocket scientist to figure out what had happened. Though domestic abuse calls were rare in this neighborhood.

Erickson pulled me aside and muttered, "She won't talk. All I've been able to get out of her is that she lives here with her boyfriend, and they got into some type of altercation."

"What's the boyfriend's name?"

"The home is owned by Armando Duarte. He doesn't appear to be here. Now she doesn't want to press charges. I told her it's not up to her anymore. Her name is Shiloh. Why don't you talk to her and see if you can get anything out of her?"

"Call Daniels. Let's put out a BOLO on the scumbag."

Erickson nodded.

I stepped back to the porch. "Ma'am, do you mind if we come inside and talk for a moment?"

She sniffled and delicately wiped her eyes. "I'm fine now. Can't you just go?"

"I'm afraid we can't do that."

"I'm gonna be in so much trouble," she said, still weeping.

"You're not in any trouble. The person who did this to you is in trouble."

"I've changed my mind. I don't want to press charges."

"That's up to the state now," I said. "You got lucky this time. The next time, you might not get so lucky."

It's pretty common for victims of domestic abuse to call the police in the heat of the moment. Then, when things settle down, they realize the gravity of the situation and want to change their mind. They want to drop the charges. And they fear retaliation from their significant other.

Shiloh hesitated for a long moment. "He doesn't mean to do it. He just..."

"Can't control himself?"

She gave a subtle nod.

"Has he ever hit you before?" I asked.

"Yeah. But never like this."

"What sparked the argument?"

She clammed up. "I don't know."

"I think you do know."

She looked beyond me to the street. The neighbors were peering through the blinds, gawking at the scene.

"I guess you guys can come inside." She stepped aside and invited us in.

Like the other homes in the Platinum Dunes Estates, there were imported marble floors and crown molding on the ceiling. Expensive furniture and fine luxury appointments.

In the foyer, there were statues of Greek gods atop pedestals. A dual staircase curved up to the second floor. There was a library to the left and a parlor to the right. It was a little gaudy and overdone—new money.

Shiloh led us into the living room. It had high vaulted ceilings typical of the neighborhood. The large windows offered a view of the pool and the canal beyond. The open area floor plan connected seamlessly to the kitchen and bar.

"Let's start at the beginning," I said. "Tell me exactly what happened."

35

"We got into an argument," Shiloh said. "Things escalated. Armando grabbed me by the throat and slammed me against the wall. He punched me a couple times and said if I ever told anyone..."

"Told anyone what?" I asked.

She hesitated. "It doesn't matter."

"It does matter."

"I really shouldn't be talking to you. You guys are cops. You'll twist around anything I say."

"Nobody's going to twist around anything," I said. "We're here to help you. How did you get away from him?"

"I apologized and pleaded with him. I told him I'd do whatever he wanted. When he let me go, I ran to the bathroom, locked myself in, and called 911."

"What started the fight?"

Shiloh didn't say anything.

"I know you're going through a range of emotions right now. And you clearly have a distrust of the police. I just want to assure you that you are not in any trouble. We just want to ensure your safety. We want to find Armando and keep him from coming back here and doing even more damage. It's okay that you're feeling conflicted. I'm sure there are a lot of positive things about your relationship, or you wouldn't still be with him."

"He's really sweet, and he's good to me, except..." She slumped. "I mean, what am I supposed to do? You guys are gonna arrest him and take him to jail. Then what? Who's gonna pay the rent on this place? I'll lose everything. I'll have to go back to stripping and move into some crappy little apartment."

"Stay with Armando long enough, and one day he's gonna take things too far. I see this all the time."

Her eyes rounded with fear. She knew it was true. Shiloh took a seat on the couch and fidgeted nervously.

JD and I took the chairs next to the sofa.

Shiloh trembled, her knee bouncing involuntarily. She took a deep breath, and with an exhale, the floodgates opened. "He was freaked out about me going to therapy. He was worried I was going to say something that I shouldn't. But I told him it's not a big deal. Talking to a therapist is like talking to a lawyer. They can't say anything. But he just couldn't understand that."

I exchanged a glance with JD. I knew where this was going. "Who's your therapist?"

"Nina Harlow."

That hung in the air like fog.

"He kept going on and on that her therapy notes could be subpoenaed. I told him she didn't take therapy notes. I told him he was overreacting. He flipped out, grabbed my throat, and shoved me against the wall."

"What was it that he didn't want you talking to Nina about?" I asked.

She clammed up again.

"Does the name Emmett Forrester sound familiar?" I asked.

Her frazzled eyes flicked to me, then she looked down again. She knew the name. No doubt about it.

"That's the guy who went missing, right?" she asked, still looking down.

"Right."

Her face tensed, and she fidgeted even more. She finally groaned, "Okay. But if I talk to you, I need you to promise I'm not gonna get in trouble."

"If you're about to tell me what I think you're about to tell me, I'm sure we can work something out."

She hesitated. "We were at *Turtles*, and Armando was being a dick. So, I started flirting with this guy to make him jealous."

"Emmett?"

"Yeah."

"Did you know him previously?"

"No. Not really. But I'd seen him out before, and I thought he was cute. Anyway, Armando flipped out and wanted to beat the shit out of the guy. I managed to calm him down and told him that this was not the time nor the place. The last thing he needed was to get arrested for brawling in a bar. He didn't need the attention. I thought I had talked some sense into him. But Armando wouldn't let it go. He dragged me out of the bar, and we waited in the parking lot for Emmett to leave. Armando followed him home and confronted him in the parking lot of his apartment complex. They got into a fight, and it all happened in seconds. Next thing I know, Emmett's dead, and Armando is rummaging through his pockets, taking his keys and wallet. He found Emmett's car and stuffed him in the trunk. Then we got out of there. I was totally freaked out, but here's the screwed up part... It kinda turned me on."

JD and I exchanged an awkward glance.

Shiloh continued, "The danger... the excitement... That's what I was seeing Nina about. I mean, we went home after that and had the most amazing sex ever! I felt guilty about it. But also thrilled by it. Then when Nina turned up dead, I knew Armando did it."

"We'll need you to come down to the station and make a sworn affidavit. You'll need to testify in court."

"What if I don't want to testify?"

"If you don't cooperate, you could be charged as a co-conspirator."

"Co-conspirator?"

"You were present during the murder, and you didn't notify the authorities. That makes you an accomplice."

Her eyes narrowed at me. "See, I knew you were gonna twist this around."

"I'm not twisting this around. I'm just telling you... make a statement saying exactly what you just told us, and you won't get in any trouble."

"But Armando will go to prison, right?"

"Where he can't hurt you."

She thought about it for a long moment.

36

"Okay," Shiloh said. "I'll testify. But you have to keep me safe."

"We will," I assured.

"And not just from Armando," she said. "He's got connections."

"What kind of connections?"

"Look around. Where do you think all of this comes from?"

"I take it he's not a legitimate businessman?"

"No. He's a fucking drug dealer."

I shared a glance with JD. We were definitely going to nail this perp.

"He works for the cartel," Shiloh continued.

"Are there any drugs at the house now?" I asked.

She shrugged. "I don't think so. He never brings it around the house. He has his crew move all the product. But he's not as big-time as he likes to think he is."

"Who's his crew?" I asked.

"Two losers. Remy and Kendrick."

"You know their last names?"

She told us, and I texted the information to Denise to see what she could find out.

"You mind if we take a look around the house?" I asked Shiloh.

"Go ahead."

The EMTs treated her while we searched the mansion looking for drugs and weapons. We didn't find any drugs, but we did find a 9mm handgun in the nightstand drawer and a sawed-off shotgun in the bedroom closet. The shotgun was an illegal weapon. The 9mm was loaded with jacketed hollow-points.

I felt reasonably certain we had our perp.

Shiloh went to the station and made a videotaped statement, and signed a sworn affidavit. Her injuries were documented with pictures and video. She seemed relieved afterward, like a weight had been lifted.

"So, how is this going to work? How long are you guys going to protect me?"

"You may be eligible for the Witness Security Program with the US Marshals. It is available to witnesses to state and federal felonies that are being threatened or may be retaliated against. It's a process, and every application is vetted by the DOJ. How much do you know about Armando's cartel connections?"

"I know a little," she said. "I know he gets a shipment every week. I know Remy and Kendrick handle the product and dispense it to the smaller dealers. They collect the cash and handle enforcement. Both Remy and Kendrick run a crew underneath them. It's like a big pyramid scheme."

"Do you know who Armando's cartel connection is?"

"A guy named Juan Valverde. Every few months or so, he comes into town, and we all go out to dinner. The guy's annoying. Loud and obnoxious, and he's always surrounded by goons. But hey, when the boss wants to take you out for dinner, you go, right?"

"Have you ever overheard them talking about business?"

"I don't know what they talk about. And half the time they talk in Spanish, and I don't understand what they're saying." She paused. "But Juan would congratulate Armando about the job he was doing. I remember there was some discussion about increasing the volume of product he was handling. There's always a weird vibe at these get-togethers. Juan and Armando were old friends, but at the same time, this was business. Juan was there to both encourage Armando, but also remind him how powerful the cartel was. Juan's security guys were always armed, and you could see it in their eyes, they were just soulless."

I was beginning to think Shiloh had more than just Armando to fear. I was pretty sure the cartel would put pressure on Armando to tie up any loose ends. Shiloh had probably seen and heard more than the cartel would have liked. And with the couple on the outs, Shiloh would be a target.

She told us some of Armando's hangouts and gave us his prepaid cellular number.

I called Isabella and asked her to track Armando's phone and give me as much information about Juan Valverde as she could find.

"It's off the grid right now," Isabella said. "It's probably turned off. I'll let you know if it pops up. I'll get back with you shortly about Juan Valverde."

The county sprang for a hotel room for Shiloh at the *Seven Seas* and posted a deputy overnight.

"Why don't you contact that acquaintance of yours at the network?" Daniels suggested to me. "I want Armando's picture on every media outlet."

"She probably already knows," I said.

I texted Paris anyway and sent Armando's mug shot from a previous DUI conviction.

Denise looked up addresses for Remy and Kendrick. Both of the goons had condos in the *Trident Tower*. It was a luxury high-rise. Armando and his crew may not have been the biggest dealers on the island, but they did okay for themselves. Remy lived on the 17th floor and Kendrick on the 15th.

We left the station with Erickson and Faulkner and headed to the *Trident*. I flashed my badge to the concierge and gained access to the lobby. We advanced to the elevators and stepped aboard when the doors opened.

JD and I hopped off on the 15th floor while Erickson and Faulkner proceeded to the 17th. This was just going to be a simple knock and talk. We'd be able to tell pretty quickly if Kendrick was harboring a fugitive.

We pushed down the hallway and knocked on #1514.

"Coconut County! We'd like to talk to you for a minute."

There was no response.

I heard commotion and footsteps down the hallway. Then the peephole flickered as someone looked through it. "What do you want?"

"We're looking for Armando Duarte. Have you seen him?"

"Nope."

"Mind if we come in and take a look around?"

"Get fucked."

"I can come back with a warrant."

"Do it."

"Armando is wanted in connection with three murders. If you're harboring a fugitive or you've aided or abetted, you will go down."

"He ain't here. I ain't got nothing to do with nothing."

"Okay. If you want to do things the hard way..."

He didn't respond.

JD and I stepped away from the door and conferred.

"I don't know about you, but I smell a strong odor of marijuana coming from that condo. That leads me to believe there's a crime in progress. I say we kick down the door."

There was no significant odor.

I shook my head, and JD frowned.

I called Sheriff Daniels to see if we could get a search warrant.

"On what probable cause?" he asked. "Has anyone seen Armando enter or exit the condo? The fact that they're acquaintances is not enough. I've already talked to the judge."

"Let's put a couple deputies on the condo and see if he shows up."

"Are you volunteering?"

I hesitated. "I would say our resources are better deployed elsewhere."

"I don't have the extra manpower. I've already got a deputy at the *Seven Seas*. I don't have any more to spare. So, if you guys want to sit on the apartment, be my guest."

I didn't much feel like sitting in this hallway all night, waiting to see if Armando emerged from the condo. There was only one way in or out of the condo unless you wanted to scale the balcony.

"Let me talk with Erickson and Faulkner," I said. "See if they found anything."

I ended the call and sent a text to Erickson. He replied an instant later. *[Nothing here. Remy opened the door, invited us in, and we looked around the apartment. No sign of Armando.]*

[It's interesting. Kendrick wouldn't even open the door.]

[We're on our way down.]

They joined us a few minutes later in the hallway.

"I've got a solution for this," JD said.

We all eyed him curiously.

He grinned. "Stay here. I'll be back shortly. He jogged down the hallway, pressed the call button on the elevator, and disappeared when the doors opened. I think I knew what he had up his sleeve.

37

J D drove home, grabbed his drone, and returned to the *Trident*. He stood in the parking lot, launched the drone into the air, counted the floors up, and navigated the unmanned aerial vehicle to the balcony of Kendrick's apartment. The drone had a 4K camera attached to a gyro stabilizer. The images were relayed to JD's phone that he mounted atop the drone's controller.

Jack piloted the vehicle onto the balcony and scanned inside the apartment, first peering into the bedroom, then into the living room.

It didn't take long for Kendrick to see the drone hovering outside his sliding glass doors. He slid open the doors, charged the device, and swatted at it.

JD navigated it away and landed the drone in the parking lot.

When it was all over, JD sent me a text message, telling me all about it. *[Unless Armando is hiding under the bed or in the closet, he's not in that condo.]*

[You're sure?]

[Reasonably so.]

[Why didn't Kendrick want to open the door?]

[Because he's got 2 keys on his coffee table. I've got video footage of him tooting on it. I recorded the whole thing. I'd say that's probable cause.]

[Nope. Freedom from Unwarranted Surveillance Act. Prohibits law enforcement agencies from using drones to gather evidence or information.]

[There are notable exceptions. 'When swift action is needed to forestall the imminent escape of a suspect.' I know the law, bitch.]

I laughed. [Send the footage to Daniels. Let's see what the judge says.]

Moments later, JD joined us on the 15th floor, and we waited eagerly for a reply.

Daniels called back 20 minutes later. "No dice."

"Why not?"

"Because there's nothing on that footage to indicate the imminent escape of a suspect. There's footage of a guy snorting a white powder. We don't know what that white powder is. Either way, it does not fall under the exemptions of the Unwarranted Surveillance Act. So stand down and either sit on the condo or pursue other leads."

"You're the boss," I said before hanging up.

There was much disappointment among us.

"Look," Faulkner said. "Armando is not gonna be dumb enough to come to either of these locations. He knows this is the first place we'll look. The guy is long gone. Plus, if he was thinking about coming here, these ass-clowns probably already called him and gave him a heads up that we're here."

He had a point.

"Maybe he's got another girlfriend?" Erickson said. "Did you consider that? Maybe that's where he is."

JD and I exchanged a curious glance.

I called Shiloh at the *Seven Seas* and asked if she knew about other women Armando may have been seeing. She groaned. "Ugh, that little whore, Gianna."

"What do you know about her?"

"I know I'd like to beat the shit out of her."

"Apart from that."

"I caught him with her once before. He was banging her in his car in the parking lot of *Forbidden Fruit*. And I know that bastard still sees her."

"Where can we find her?"

"I don't know. But I have my suspicions that he pays for her apartment."

"What's Gianna's last name?"

"Silver."

I hung up, called Denise, and asked her to look up the information. Gianna's current residence was listed at 3405 Moray Way, #205 in the *Delphine Apartments*. We left the *Trident* and headed across town. I figured it was a long shot.

We banged on the door of the mid-rise apartment. There was no response. We knocked a few more times, and still no answer.

It gave us a good excuse to go to *Forbidden Fruit* on *official business.*

The upscale adult establishment on Oyster Avenue always provided a visual feast. Slender beauties slinked around chrome poles. Fog billowed from stages as spotlights slashed the air, highlighting the scantily clad performers. There were spike-heeled shoes, tight curves, and frilly lingerie. Bodies shimmered in the light, and hair flipped. The girls displayed amazing flexibility and physical prowess. Climbing up a pole and spinning around like an acrobat takes skill and strength.

Music pumped through speakers, and a DJ with a deep, soothing voice announced dancers as they took the stage. The place smelled like whiskey and cheap perfume mixed with the residue of glycol fog. Bills were stuffed in G-strings, and girls undulated in ways designed to separate the predominantly male patrons from their cash.

We stepped inside and glanced around. The manager, Jaco, leaned against the main bar. He wore a shiny gray sharkskin suit and a black shirt.

We headed toward him, and he greeted us with a smile. "If it isn't my two favorite deputies," he said in a tone that was mostly sincere. Our investigations took us to *Forbidden Fruit* quite frequently, and we never leaned on Jaco or hassled him, unlike some other county officials. "Is this business or pleasure?

"Looking for Gianna Silver?"

He pointed to a brunette vixen who gave an impressive lap dance to a satisfied customer.

Gianna oozed sexuality, and her body rippled and writhed in enticing ways as she danced.

"Her stage name is Houston," Jaco said.

I pulled up a picture of Armando's mugshot on my phone and showed it to him. "Have you seen this guy in here before?"

"Yeah. He's in all the time. I think he's got a thing with Gianna."

"Has he been in lately?" I asked.

I haven't seen him in about a week. "What did he do?"

"We're looking at him for the murder of three people, among other things."

Jaco lifted his brow. "Impressive. You want me to call Gianna over here?"

"No. And don't tell her we're asking around."

"Gotcha," Jaco said with a wink. "Undercover surveillance. I like it."

"If Armando turns up, call me."

"You got it," Jaco said.

We meandered through the dim club and took a seat away from the stage. We kept a watchful eye on Gianna.

"Now, this is the kind of stakeout that I can get on board with," JD said.

38

J aco sent us a round of drinks on the house. We surveilled Gianna for the rest of the evening and may have been forced to receive a few lap dances to maintain our cover.

After the club closed, we followed Gianna back to her apartment like a couple of stalkers. I had called Isabella and asked her to monitor Armando's phone. So far, she couldn't find any indication that Gianna had been contacted by Armando. He was staying off the grid and remained elusive.

We hung out across the street from the *Delphine*, sitting in the convertible, waiting to see if Armando would show up at some point.

JD hopped out of the car and pulled the drone from the front trunk of the Porsche. He launched the craft and piloted it close to Gianna's balcony, peering inside with the 4K camera. A quick survey of the living room and the bedroom didn't reveal anything but Gianna undressing for bed—which we already had seen plenty of at *Forbidden Fruit*.

JD piloted the drone back to the Porsche, packed it in its case, and put it back into the trunk. We hung out until the wee hours of the morning, and Armando never did show his face. I was beginning to think he was long gone.

I asked Isabella to keep tabs on Gianna's phone in case Armando tried to contact her.

We called it a night and drove back to *Diver Down*. JD dropped me off in the lot, and I told him I'd talk to him in the morning. I ambled down the dock toward the *Avventura*, still cautious that Phoebe might be lurking in the shadows.

I decided to go ahead and unblock her number. I cringed as I did so, expecting a flurry of text messages at any moment thereafter. But it was late. Well after 3 AM. And my phone remained silent.

I crossed the passerelle to the aft deck, slid open the salon door, and stepped inside. Buddy lifted his sleepy head from the settee, where he was curled up. I greeted him and took him for a late-night walk before settling into bed.

I woke up in the morning, and much to my surprise, there were no text messages on my phone. No nasty voicemails. Maybe Phoebe moved on as quickly as she had become fixated. That was my hope anyway. I really didn't mean to hurt her feelings. It was just too much, too soon.

I still hadn't heard anything from Isabella about Armando. All the networks were reporting about the fugitive, asking viewers to call the Sheriff's Department if they had any information.

After breakfast, I took Buddy for a walk. On the way back to the boat, Daniels called. "I need you and numb-nuts to get down to the station."

"What's up?"

"Those pirates struck again."

"Is anybody hurt?"

"I don't think so."

"On my way."

I called JD and told him I'd meet him at the station. I rushed back to the *Avventura*, grabbed my helmet and gloves, and sprinted to my sportbike. I pulled on my gear, straddled the crotch rocket, and cranked up the engine. The exhaust rattled and howled as I twisted the throttle and eased out the clutch. I launched out of the parking lot and hugged the tank, racing down the road. It was like trying to hold on to a rocket that had been launched toward the moon. Instant adrenaline. The wind whistled through my helmet.

I pulled into the lot at the station, parked the bike, and jogged down the dock to the patrol boat.

JD arrived moments later, and we cast off the lines. Daniels took the helm, and we idled out of the harbor. He brought the boat on plane, and the aluminum hull carved through the swells.

"That pistol you took from Armando's residence is a match in the Nina Harlow case," Daniels said. "I can say with certainty that gun killed her and Sebastian."

At least we were on the right track. Now, all we had to do was find the scumbag.

We caught up with a superyacht that had been anchored near Barracuda Key island. It was a 131' *Benini*. A sleek Italian vessel with expert craftsmanship and opulent appointments.

We pulled alongside the swim platform and boarded the superyacht. The owner, Charles Anthony, greeted us on the aft deck with wide eyes, still trembling. He had reddish hair, a round face, and a healthy belly.

His girlfriend was a young blonde. She was in the salon pouring vodka into a glass, trembling. She was putting them down as fast as possible.

"Thank God you're here!" Charles said.

"What happened?" I asked.

We spent the night out here last night and were enjoying a nice breakfast when the Coast Guard came along and wanted to board us. I didn't think anything of it until they boarded with machine guns and demanded our valuables. Then I realized they weren't the Coast Guard."

So far, this was sounding exactly like the group of marauders that I had encountered previously.

"How many were there?" I asked.

"4. They all wore tactical gear, and their faces were covered. One guy was clearly the leader. Seemed like a nice enough guy, except for the fact he had a gun in my face. I don't know about you, but I have an aversion to being on the wrong end of an assault rifle. He said if we cooperated, nobody would get hurt. They just wanted the valuables."

"What did they take?"

"My watch, her diamond necklace and earrings. They took the cash from my wallet, a couple guns from my stateroom, my 1959 Les Paul guitar..."

JD cringed. The classic instrument was worth upwards of a quarter-million dollars.

"... and my Picasso."

"You own a Picasso?" I asked.

"Yeah. It was a sketch. But still, not cheap."

"Then what happened?"

"They loaded up the loot and left. I called you boys."

"Can you describe any of the assailants?"

He shook his head. "Like I said. They all wore face coverings."

"Who knew about the Picasso?"

He shrugged. "Anybody that has been on board. It's one of my favorite pieces. I like to show it off to everybody. But I don't think that's what they were after. I think they got lucky. The guitar is worth more than the Picasso. I only paid $65,000 for the sketch."

"A bargain," JD said dryly.

"I thought so."

Charles filled out a report, and we escorted the superyacht back to Coconut Key. Charles was understandably a little skittish about being on the water.

After we filled out after-action reports, I hopped on the bike, and JD followed me back to *Diver Down*. We pushed into the restaurant and took a seat at the bar.

Teagan greeted us with her usual cheery smile. "Rough morning?"

"Whatever gave you that idea?" I asked.

"I don't know. I just got a bad feeling. It's like I'm waiting for the other shoe to drop."

When Teagan got a bad feeling, it was usually something to listen to. Maybe her *on again, off again* psychic powers were coming back?

39

"He just called, and boy, is he pissed off," Shiloh said, her voice crackling through the speaker in my phone.

Shiloh was still at the *Seven Seas* under the protection of a deputy.

"What did he say?" I asked.

"Oh, he threatened to kill me," she said casually. "Par for the course with Armando."

"That's good."

"What!?"

"If he calls again, keep antagonizing him. Maybe we can draw him out."

"You want to use me as bait? Hell no. Have you lost your mind?"

"Do you know where he was calling from?"

"I don't know where he was, but he called from his prepaid cellular."

Isabella called me on the other line. "Thanks. I'll call you right back." I switched over.

"Armando's burner phone just popped up on the grid and called Shiloh."

"I know."

"He's at the FBO at the Coconut Key airport. You better hurry if you want to catch him. Looks like he turned on his phone long enough to make the call. It's off the grid again."

I called Sheriff Daniels as we raced out of the bar and hopped into JD's Porsche. He cranked up the engine, dropped the car into gear, and left a streak of rubber across the asphalt as we peeled out of the parking lot. Wind swirled about the cabin as we dashed to the FBO.

We screeched into the private terminal, and JD parked the car at the curb. We raced inside, displaying our badges.

The 3,000 square-foot, two-story terminal at the FBO was a luxury lounge for the rich and famous as they waited for their departures. There was a conference room, a café, and restrooms—though the terminal rarely saw much traffic. Most travelers were chauffeured onto the tarmac by limousine. They'd hop out and climb aboard their aircraft.

Unlike traditional flights, private jets weren't subject to the rules of the TSA. There were no security screenings. No tickets. Pilots still had to file flight plans, and passengers had to provide ID or passport, but there were no restrictions on baggage or pets. None of the hassles of commercial air travel. The 12,000 square-foot hangar at the FBO could accommodate *Slipstream G750s* with ease.

A jet raced down the tarmac as we entered the terminal. It lifted into the air and retracted its gear, nosing skyward.

I had a sinking feeling that Armando was aboard that aircraft.

I raced to the desk and asked the attendant where the flight was going and who was aboard.

"I believe the flight is heading to Mexico." She looked up the flight plan and passenger manifest. "There is a single passenger on board. David Smith."

My face twisted with confusion. I was pretty sure Armando would be traveling under an alias. There was no doubt he had a fake passport. I pulled up Armando's mugshot on my phone and showed it to the associate. "You recognize this man?"

She studied it carefully. "Yeah. That's him. The cab dropped him off out front. He walked through the terminal, onto the tarmac, and boarded the plane."

My jaw tensed. The son-of-a-bitch got away, and there was no telling where he was really headed.

"We can always make a trip to Mexico," JD muttered in my ear. "Take care of this the old-fashioned way."

That was not my first choice.

I called Sheriff Daniels and updated him on the situation. His efforts to ground the flights out of the FBO had obviously failed. Daniels contacted the Mexican authorities and put out an international warrant for Armando Duarte, traveling under the alias of David Smith.

I wasn't holding my breath.

Sometimes you got cooperation at the border, and sometimes you didn't. If Armando had cartel ties, he was long gone. The cartels had everyone on their payroll. They would pay law enforcement officers more in a month than they would make in an entire year from their regular salary. The corruption was rampant and reached the highest levels of government.

Maybe JD was right. Maybe if we wanted Armando to face justice, we'd have to go down there and bring him back ourselves.

I knew JD would want to finish the job while we were there and save the taxpayers money, but I was trying not to use lethal force unless absolutely necessary. I had a deep-seated belief that I'd been given a second chance at life for the explicit purpose of doing my part to make the world a better place. Indiscriminately assassinating baddies seemed to be slightly at odds with my core premise. There needed to be some sense of *just cause*.

In my years as a clandestine operative, the phrase *the end justifies the means* was quite often used as justification for less than scrupulous activities. Sometimes, you had to do what you had to do. But it was a slippery slope. Soon, you could find yourself justifying all types of things for the *greater good*. I never wanted to go down that slippery path again. I wasn't against breaking a few laws here and there to get the job done, but by and large, I wanted to serve justice honorably. I wanted to sleep well at night, and when my time was all said and done, I never wanted to go back to hell. Once was enough.

We left the airport and headed back across town. JD had band practice in the afternoon, and I tagged along.

We pulled into the parking lot of the practice studio, and the usual group of miscreants was out front, smoking cigarettes and other things.

"Sup, Thrash?" one of them asked, high-fiving JD as he passed.

"Living the dream," JD said. "Living the dream."

We pushed into the dim hallway and got a nice whiff of a potent herbal scent. We stepped into the practice space as the band was tuning up. Haphazard notes rang out as Dizzy and Crash tuned their guitars. Styxx tapped the drum heads as he tuned and positioned them just how he wanted them.

As usual, there were a couple groupies on the couch. I took a seat next to the lovely ladies and kicked back for the show. The band ran through their set, which was familiar by now.

People started piling into the room for a free show. Every practice turned into a small gig.

Styxx pounded on the drums, Dizzy's fingers streaked up and down the fretboard, and Crash laid down the groove on bass. JD pranced around, howling into the microphone, flipping his mane of hair like he was on the stage at Madison Square Garden.

It didn't matter where *Wild Fury* played. It was all or nothing, even in practice. It was more than music. It was an attitude. A take no prisoners, grab you by the throat and never

let go rock 'n' roll band. The kind of band that's almost
extinct now. And maybe that's why they were so well
received.

And I was their manager.

It was a Tuesday night, and after practice, the band was
more than ready to continue the party. It was like they were
on a world tour that never left Coconut Key.

We shifted the party to *Tide Pool*, and JD picked up the bill.
Fans crowded around the rockers, and JD kept them enter-
tained with stories and shots. It was a little after 11 PM when
Teagan called me. "Hey, can you come over?"

This wasn't an invitation for something naughty. There was
panic in her voice.

"What's wrong?"

40

"Where are you?" I asked.

"I'm at my apartment," Teagan replied. "I got off at 9 PM, and Alejandro took over. He's working till close at the bar. Some guy followed me home. He just came to the door and banged on it. I didn't answer. I don't know if he is still out there."

"You have your gun handy?"

"It's in my purse."

"I'll be right over."

I told JD I was going to check on Teagan. I didn't tell him she had a stalker. I let him bask in his rockstar glory.

I caught a ride-share to Teagan's apartment and rang her from the call box in the lobby. She buzzed me in, and I took the elevator up to her floor.

There was no one in the hallway.

I stayed on the phone with her the whole time and told her it was me knocking on the door and not to shoot.

She pulled the door open a moment later with panicked eyes. I stepped inside the foyer, and she closed the door behind me and latched the deadbolt.

"This isn't some ploy to get me alone and take advantage of me, is it?" I asked.

She shot me a look. "No. I'm serious. You don't understand, ever since that video, I've had to block so many freaks on social media. I swear, this guy has been following me around for days. I kept feeling like I was seeing the same guy in my periphery."

"When he knocked on the door, did he say anything?"

"No. I wasn't about to go near the door and ask who it was. I just didn't respond."

"I didn't see anybody in the lobby or in the hallway," I said.

"He could be lurking in the stairwell or on another floor."

"Do you know how he got into the building?"

"You know how easy it is to get around the security here."

All you had to do was wait for someone else to exit or enter, or call some random number and say you were delivering a pizza. Most people would buzz you in.

"Thanks for coming," Teagan said in a soft voice. "I'm so freaked out." She grabbed my hand. "Feel my heart. It's beating a million miles a minute."

She placed my hand on her chest, perilously close to her sumptuous cleavage. Her heart thumped against my palm.

I figured I better remove my hand before it *accidentally* slipped. I think my heart started beating a little faster, too.

"Do you think I could crash in one of the guest staterooms tonight? I'm never gonna be able to sleep here."

I gave her a suspicious gaze. "If you promise to behave yourself."

She scoffed. "Me? You're the one who is a bad influence."

My brow lifted incredulously. "Okay. Whatever."

"I can't help it if you're hopelessly attracted to me. It's not my fault."

I rolled my eyes.

"And believe me. I'm not going anywhere near you after you've been with that psycho chick." She paused. "Have you heard any more from her?"

"Not since she was waiting at JD's car for us on Oyster Avenue."

Teagan's brow lifted, and her jaw dropped. "She really *is* stalking you. You must have some good stuff if she got hooked after two days."

"I have my redeeming qualities," I said with a grin. "Why don't you get together some things, and we'll head back to the marina?"

She smiled. "Yay! I really appreciate you looking after me."

"That's what friends are for."

I waited while Teagan gathered a change of clothes and put together an overnight kit. When she was ready, we pushed down the foyer, and I unlatched the door. I kept a wary hand on the grip of my pistol, ready to draw it from its holster at a moment's notice. I pulled open the door and looked in either direction down the hallway.

It was clear.

I ushered Teagan out of the apartment, and she locked the door behind us. We rushed down the hallway to the elevator and pressed the call button. Teagan fidgeted as we waited for the lift to arrive.

I kept a watchful eye on the stairwells at either end of the hallway.

The doors slid open, and we stepped inside. I think Teagan got even more freaked out in the claustrophobic space. We plummeted down to the first floor. The doors opened, and I poked my head out and scanned in all directions.

The lobby was clear.

I shuffled Teagan out of the elevator, and we waited in the lobby until the ride-share arrived. Then we rushed down the sidewalk to the curb and hopped into the car.

Teagan breathed a sigh of relief once we were on our way back to the marina.

The drama for the night wasn't over. As we walked along the dock to the *Avventura*, it became clear I had a visitor. Phoebe waited on the aft deck. Rage filled her eyes when she saw Teagan. Her anger was compounded by the fact that Teagan had baggage and was clearly spending the night.

Phoebe went into a tirade. "I knew it. How long have you been fucking her behind my back?"

I was stunned at her inability to grasp reality. "Whoa! Hang on a minute. There is no *behind your back*. Phoebe, you're out of line. You need to leave. Now."

"You're the one who's out of line!" she screeched.

Teagan took shelter behind me.

"You're trespassing. You need to leave."

"I'm trespassing? That's rich. She's the one who's trespassing. She needs to get her own man."

There was no reasoning with her.

"Maybe I shouldn't stay here tonight," Teagan whispered.

"No. It's fine. I'll handle this," I said to Teagan, then addressed Phoebe. "I understand you're upset, and I'm sorry if you feel I led you on in any way. But it's over. And it's beyond repair. Now, please leave."

She snarled like a demon. "You think I'm going to let you use me like a cheap whore and get away with it?"

I had enough of the nonsense, and the situation had the potential to go terribly wrong. I pulled out my phone and called the Sheriff's Department. "This is Deputy Wild. Could you send a patrol unit to the marina at *Diver Down?* There's a trespasser on my property."

Phoebe's eyes bulged with anger, and she looked like she was about to explode. "You just made a big mistake."

"Oh, really? How so?"

Her eyes narrowed, and she seethed with anger. "Oh, just wait. You can't fuck me over like this and get away with it."

"Nobody is screwing anybody over, Phoebe. I'm sorry if there was a misunderstanding between us."

She clenched her jaw and fumed.

The patrol car pulled into the parking lot and spun up the red and blue lights, cascading a wash of color over the marina.

"Looks like your ride is here," I said.

Phoebe glared at me. She did not like my *one-liner* one bit. She stormed across the passerelle to the dock, and we gave her a wide berth. "You're seriously going to have me arrested?"

"I asked you politely to leave."

"You're going to regret this." Her face twisted, and she snarled again. She charged at me, fists flailing, pounding my chest.

Erickson and Faulkner rushed down the dock, having seen the attack.

I grabbed Phoebe's arms and kept her from punching me. The deputies pulled her away and cuffed her.

She screeched a slew of obscenities, practically frothing at the mouth.

The deputies dragged her down the dock and stuffed her in the back of the patrol car, kicking and screaming.

Phoebe was unhinged.

I escorted Teagan aboard the *Avventura* and unlocked the salon door. She was already frazzled, and this didn't help. I told her I'd be back momentarily and to make herself at home.

I jogged down the dock to the parking lot and caught up with the deputies. It was all they could do to keep from laughing their asses off.

"What's the matter, Wild? She too much for you to handle?" Erickson said with a snicker.

"I thought it best to have other officers present, given the situation."

I was never going to live this down. They would tease me incessantly.

"What the hell did you do to her?" Faulkner asked.

"Nothing. I swear!"

"You sure can pick 'em, Wild," Erickson said.

Faulkner said, "All joking aside, I witnessed her assault you. She already has two trespassing charges on file."

I paused. I didn't want to do it, but this was out of control. "Book her on trespassing and assault. Let her spend the night in jail. Maybe that will calm her down. If the harassment stops, I'll drop the charges."

Faulkner shrugged. "Whatever you say."

They climbed into the patrol car and pulled away.

Phoebe glared at me through the window, her scornful eyes throwing daggers.

I hustled back down the dock to the *Avventura*. Teagan waited for me in the salon.

"Geez, Tyson. That was freaky. That girl is dangerous."

"A night in jail ought to put things in perspective."

"She has a history of this type of behavior. I don't think a night in jail is going to do anything to deter her. You need to get a restraining order."

"That's not going to do much good either," I said.

"Yeah, but it's something."

I didn't want to admit it, but it was becoming a problem.

"Where do you want me?" Teagan asked.

That would normally have been a loaded question, but we were both in a different state of mind.

"There are plenty of guest rooms. Take your pick—except the VIP on the main deck. That's Jack's."

I escorted Teagan below deck and showed her the offerings. She selected a queen berth with a private en suite. I left her to get settled and told her I was going to the galley to fix a sandwich. I asked her if she wanted any midnight rations. She said she'd be up in a minute.

I had some lunch meat in the fridge and made a couple of chicken sandwiches on whole wheat. We talked about the crazy events of the evening. We shared a few nervous laughs once the tension had dissipated.

"I'm still a little wound up," Teagan said. "I don't think I can sleep. You want to watch a movie or something?"

"Sure."

We moved up to the theater room on the bridge deck and reclined in comfy leather chairs that leaned all the way back. Buddy joined us as we streamed a movie.

Teagan fell asleep halfway through. I found a blanket and covered her up. I debated whether I should let her sleep in the chair or wake her up.

"Hey, sleepyhead. Do you want to go to your room, or do you want to stay here all night?"

She groaned and kept her eyes closed. She mumbled, "I'm not asleep."

I laughed.

"Yes, you are."

"I'll get up in a minute."

I left her in the theater room and kept the aisle lighting on so she could get around if she got up in the middle of the night. I moved aft down the passageway to my stateroom, brushed my teeth, and climbed in bed.

It was a crazy evening, and I had never experienced anything quite like it. Phoebe's view of reality was so warped, it made you question your own sanity.

When I peeled open my eyes in the morning, I found something I didn't expect. Teagan had stumbled into my stateroom at some point during the night and curled up next to me.

She was a pleasant sight.

Teagan had peeled out of her clothes, and they were in a jumble on the deck. She still wore her bra and panties, the sheets half covering her luscious form. She was like a dessert tray at a fancy restaurant—the kind where you want to sample every delight.

I resisted the urge to snuggle up and see what developed.

Isabella called as the morning sun slipped through the windows. I grabbed the phone from the nightstand and held it to my ear. "It seems like your friend resurfaced."

"Armando? Where?" I asked in a scratchy voice.

42

I climbed out of bed and finished the call in another compartment so as not to disturb Teagan.

"Looks like Armando is in Playa," Isabella said. "His phone popped up on the grid long enough to call his girlfriend. I suppose he'll ditch that phone soon and acquire another one, but I'll keep tabs on Shiloh's line and monitor the incoming calls."

"I appreciate that."

"I know you do."

"Also, I got info on Juan Valverde. He's a mid-level cartel guy. Runs a club in Mexico. He's a frequent visitor to the States. So far, the DEA can't get anything on him, but it's clear he handles stateside operations in Coconut Key. The guy is clever. Looks like he's moving money around with a series of shell corporations. Also, I did some research on the tail number of the plane that Armando flew out on. It's registered out of Aruba, and I can't determine actual ownership.

But I'd bet you it belongs to the cartel, and they facilitated Armando's exit."

"Shiloh says they're old friends."

"Friends or not, something tells me they don't want Armando in custody, and they certainly don't want him talking about the operation. I'm sure you already know this, but Shiloh is going to be a high-priority target for them. So, stay frosty."

"Always."

"I'll keep you posted," she said before ending the call.

I called Shiloh.

"I was just about to call you," she said.

"I know you spoke with Armando. What did he say?"

"The usual. He swore up and down he was going to kill me. That he was going to come back when I least expected it. He said he would make my death slow and painful. I told him that summed up my entire time with him. Just to rattle his cage, I told him I was going to fuck all his friends and everyone he knew."

I laughed. "How did he take that?"

"It was kind of comical, actually. He just went off screaming. So, I hung up on him." She paused. "Do you really think he's stupid enough to come back here and try something?"

"I don't know. Some people just can't control themselves. They let anger cloud their judgment. Have you talked to anybody else since you've been at the *Seven Seas*? Friends, family?"

"I called Cassidy. Why?"

"Did you tell her where you were staying?"

"Yeah."

I groaned.

"What's the big deal. She's not going to tell Armando."

"Is the deputy still outside your room?"

"Yeah, I think so. Do you want me to check?"

"Call through the door and see if he's still there, but do not open the door for anyone."

"Okay, hang on..."

Shiloh put the phone down and moved to the door. I heard her shout to the Deputy outside. "Are you still there?"

"Yes, ma'am."

She returned to the phone a moment later. "He's still there. Everything's fine. Relax."

"I need Cassidy's number."

"Okay. I'll text it to you."

"Stay put. Don't leave the room."

"Yes, Boss," she mocked.

The contact info buzzed my phone a moment later, and I called Cassidy. The phone rang a few times, then went to voicemail. I left a message and asked her to return my call as soon as possible.

I called Sheriff Daniels. "Operational security has been compromised. I think we should move Shiloh over to the Hyton."

He groaned. "What part of *don't contact anyone* do these people not understand?" He let out an exasperated sigh. "Deputy Pierce is standing watch at the *Seven Seas*. Go over there and escort the girl to another location. This time make sure she doesn't tell anyone where she is. Take away her damn cell phone."

"You got it."

"Oh, by the way, your girlfriend was arraigned this morning. She bonded out. Just thought you might like to know."

"She's not my girlfriend."

"Seems like she doesn't know that."

I left a note for Teagan that I had to leave, then grabbed my helmet and gloves. I jogged to the parking lot, hopped on my bike, and cruised to the *Seven Seas*.

Shiloh was staying in Suite #317. I'd specifically instructed the deputies not to put her in a bungalow for security reasons.

Deputy Pierce stood outside the door, looking bored out of his mind. He was excited to see a familiar face. We greeted each other with a handshake.

"Daniels called, said we're moving the girl," Pierce said.

I nodded and banged on the door. "Shiloh? It's Deputy Wild."

There was no answer.

I knocked again, starting to grow concerned. "Shiloh. Open the door."

43

S hiloh finally pulled open the door with an agitated look on her face. "Geez. Chill out. I was in the bathroom."

I breathed a sigh of relief. "Pack your things. Change of venue."

I had barely gotten the words out when the snap of a suppressed bullet echoed down the hallway.

The copper round tore through the air and smacked into Deputy Pierce's head with a wet slap. It drilled through one side of his skull and blasted out the other, painting the walls, and myself, with everything that made Deputy Pierce who he was.

His lifeless body collapsed to the carpet as two gunmen closed in—one on either end of the hallway. They wore ski masks, and their stealthy barrels spit fury in my direction. Bullets crisscrossed the passageway, zipping past my ears, smacking into the wall. Plumes of gypsum erupted from the impacts.

I pushed into the hotel room and slammed the door behind me, latching the deadbolt. I ushered Shiloh to the far end of the room and had her take cover on the floor behind the bed near the balcony.

I took a position behind the solid wood desk and aimed my weapon at the doorway. I called Sheriff Daniels and apprised him of the situation. "I need backup, now!"

The goons were at the doorway and unleashed a torrent of bullets into the locking mechanism. The door rattled and quaked as they kicked it, shaking the walls, vibrating the mirrors on the sliding doors to the closet. It didn't take long before the door gave way and swung open, shards of wood splintering in all directions.

With a goon lined up in my sights, I squeezed the trigger multiple times, the weapon hammering against my palm. Muzzle flash flickered from the barrel. The sharp smell of gunpowder filled my nose as the deafening report echoed throughout the small room. If anybody was sleeping in on this floor, they weren't now.

A volley of gunfire erupted. Bullets whizzed across the room, smacking walls, paintings, and the flatscreen display. Glass popped and crackled as bullets pelted the sliding glass doors to the balcony. Glimmering shards rained down.

My bullets took out the first goon, punching cavernous holes into his chest. Blood spewed as he tumbled back. He writhed on the floor in agony as his partner took cover around the doorframe.

We exchanged a few more volleys, and I drilled several rounds into the drywall, hoping to penetrate the other side.

A moment later, I heard his footsteps stomp against the carpet as he retreated down the hall.

The desk that I had crouched behind had multiple bullets embedded into the wood.

My ears rang.

I looked at Shiloh, trembling on the carpet, half underneath the bed. "Are you okay?"

"I think so." Her face was pale, and her eyes wide.

I glanced over her body, looking for any signs of trauma. She seemed okay.

I advanced to the door and kicked the pistol out of reach of the fallen goon. It spiraled across the carpet into the hallway. I peered down the corridor to see his comrade hobble away.

I knelt down and pulled off the ski mask from the fallen goon.

It was Kendrick.

The goon running down the hallway must have been Remy.

I clipped him pretty good because there was a steady stream of blood staining the carpet. He aimed over his shoulder and fired two more shots at me.

I ducked back into the hotel room as the bullets exploded near the door frame.

The thug pushed into the stairwell. The metal door clinked, then slammed shut behind him.

Erickson and Faulkner stepped off the elevator and raced toward me.

"Look after Shiloh," I shouted, then I took off down the hall, chasing after the perp.

Curious guests began to crack open their doors and peer into the corridor. I shouted for everyone to stay inside their rooms as I ran down the hallway.

I reached the steel fire door to the stairwell and cautiously pushed inside. The echo of the thug's footsteps filled the stairway as he plummeted below. I leaned over the railing and saw him spiral down the switchback staircase.

I plunged down the steps, chasing after him as fast as I could. My heart pounded, and I skipped down the steps, trying not to bust my ass or turn an ankle.

At the first floor, the goon pushed into the lobby. I reached the landing not far behind him, then followed.

He twisted around and aimed his pistol at me. His shirt was soaked with blood, he clutched the wound with one hand. He squeezed the trigger multiple times, and several bullets rocketed from the suppressor. They snapped across the lobby like angry hornets with a helluva sting.

44

Guests in the lobby shrieked in horror as they witnessed the shocking scene. They darted for cover behind furniture.

I squeezed the trigger and pumped two rounds into the thug, finishing the job. He fell to the tile with a thump, and blood erupted from the gaping wounds in his chest. His grip went slack, and his weapon clattered away.

I rushed toward him and arrived just as the last gasp of breath rattled from his lungs. I pulled off his ski mask, and sure enough, it was Remy.

There was no doubt in my mind that Armando had ordered them to kill Shiloh, probably at the behest of the cartel bosses. Shiloh had become a liability. The fact that she had antagonized Armando only sweetened the pot.

Soon the place was swarming with deputies and first responders. Stunned guests gawked at the horrific scene as hotel staff and management tried to calm them. I'm pretty sure that all the guests that witnessed the shooting got comped a free weekend at the hotel. The manager repeatedly assured the guests that this type of activity wasn't usual —though this hadn't been the first time an assassination attempt had taken place at the posh hotel.

I gave Daniels a recap of the situation when he arrived. Erickson and Faulkner took a frazzled Shiloh to the station, where she made a statement about the events.

The forensics team snapped photos and chronicled evidence, pulling slugs from walls and from the desk inside Shiloh's hotel room. The place was trashed. It looked like a rock 'n' roll band had ravaged it. Brenda examined the bodies, and they were taken to the morgue.

There was a somber mood among the deputies as Pierce's body was rolled out on a gurney.

"You find the son-of-a-bitch behind this," Daniels said to me. "I don't care what you have to do."

After we wrapped up at the scene, the cleaning staff had the unenviable job of putting the room back together. It wouldn't be ready for guests for quite some time.

I headed to the station and filled out an after-action report. I surrendered my weapon for evaluation. It was protocol to be put on administrative leave, but that usually didn't last more than a day. The typical *investigation* into an officer-involved shooting consisted of Daniels looking over the evidence and, more often than not, clearing the deputy.

Daniels told me to take the rest of the day off and make the standard appointment with the head shrinker. "Go home. Relax. Get your head clear."

"My head *is* clear."

"You know the drill."

I was used to it by now.

"That's not gonna be the last attempt they make on Shiloh," I said.

"I know," Daniels said.

I left the station and headed back to *Diver Down*. I pulled into the lot, parked the bike, and strolled the dock to the *Avventura*. I called JD and told him what happened.

Adrenaline still coursed through my veins. I was ready for a hot shower and a cold drink. JD suggested a night out on the town to blow off steam.

"I'll consider it," I said. "I'll give you a shout later."

I wasn't much in the mood.

"I'm telling you, nothing more relaxing than a little lady to soothe your troubles. I'm sure we can find a few willing companions."

"I'll take that under advisement," I said. Though my recent experience with a particular lady had been anything but relaxing.

I noticed something odd as I strolled the dock.

Buddy was out wandering by himself. I glanced around, looking for Teagan, figuring she might have taken him out. But I didn't see her anywhere.

I told Jack I'd call him back, then knelt down and petted Buddy. "How did you get out, boy?"

The little Jack Russell followed me back to the boat. We crossed the gangway and stepped to the aft deck. I pulled open the sliding door and stepped into the salon, and I knew instantly something was wrong.

Buddy took off running.

I could smell the faint traces of perfume in the air.

It wasn't Teagan's perfume.

45

B uddy raced across the salon, his paws clattering against the deck. He darted up the steps.

I followed.

He arrived on the scene before I did, and his snarling and growling confirmed my suspicions. By the time I reached my stateroom, Buddy bared his fangs, barking incessantly at Phoebe.

She held Teagan at gunpoint—with one of my guns, no less.

"Phoebe, how about you put the gun down?" I suggested carefully.

Her face was tortured, and her eyes crazed. Her hair was disheveled, and after a night in jail, she looked like she'd been through the ringer. "If you just tell me the truth, I could forgive you. Just admit that you slept with her, and we can work through this."

Buddy kept snarling and barking.

"Buddy, stay!" The last thing I needed was for the situation to escalate. I grabbed him by the collar and held him back. I didn't want him to get shot by the crazed maniac.

I coaxed him into the en suite and closed the hatch, putting him out of harm's way.

"Phoebe, there's nothing going on here. I'm gonna ask you again to put the gun down."

Her unsteady hand kept it aimed at Teagan. She lay in the bed, and I'm sure to the casual observer it looked like we had hooked up the night before.

"Phoebe, point the gun at me," I said.

"I'm not going to let her get in between us," Phoebe shrieked.

"There's nothing between us, Phoebe. Point the gun at me. Let's talk through this."

"I know you love me. We are meant to be together. Nothing's going to keep us apart."

I decided to use a different tactic. "You're absolutely right. The only thing that is gonna keep us apart is you," I said, playing into her delusion.

Her face twisted with confusion.

"If you hurt her, you'll go to jail," I said. "How could we ever be together?"

Phoebe thought for a moment.

"You're right," I said. "I made a huge mistake. I'm sorry. I don't know how I couldn't see it before. You're definitely the one for me." I tried to sound sincere.

Her face softened for a moment, then it twisted again with rage. "You're lying. You'll say anything to save your precious little whore. You're all the same!"

She swung the barrel of the pistol around to me. I wasn't thrilled to be on the business end of it, but better me than Teagan.

"You said we could work through this," I said in a delicate tone. Calm and soothing. "Let's talk. Put the gun down."

"Stop telling me what to do!"

"I know you don't want to hurt me. How could we be together then?"

I knew I was in trouble when she said, "We could be together forever."

Tears spilled down her cheeks, and her finger tightened around the trigger.

Bam!

Bam!

The deafening bang rattled the stateroom, and Buddy howled and wailed in the en suite.

A look of terror washed over Phoebe's face. Her blouse blossomed with crimson. Her eyes swirled, and the pistol dropped from her hand, clattering the deck. She followed, collapsing to a sack of bones.

Teagan sat up in bed holding her pistol, smoke still wafting from the barrel. She had pulled the weapon from her purse on the nightstand, and just as she had trained, squeezed two rounds that hit Phoebe's center mass.

Teagan's eyes were wide, and she trembled. She set the gun down on the bed, and I advanced toward Phoebe, kicking the weapon away for good measure. I knelt down and felt for a pulse, but she was gone.

I looked at Teagan. "Are you okay?"

She nodded. "I can't believe I did that."

"Everything's gonna be okay," I assured her.

I called Sheriff Daniels and told him to send Brenda and a forensics team. It wasn't long before the *Avventura* was swarming with deputies and county officials.

We made statements, and the team took photographs and documented the evidence. No charges would be filed against Teagan, but it would take some time for her to come to grips with the situation. Taking someone's life is never easy, even when your survival depends on it.

After the circus left, I cleaned up, trying to get the blood-stains off the deck and the bulkheads.

"Is it too early to start drinking," Teagan asked.

I chuckled. "It's 5 o'clock somewhere."

I finished up in the stateroom, and we moved down to the main deck salon. I poured us both a glass of whiskey.

"Nice shooting."

"Well, I certainly wasn't gonna let her kill you. I'd be out of a job," she said dryly.

I forced a grim smile. Teagan was taking the whole thing in stride.

"Did you see that coming?"

She shook her head. "I've been getting bad vibes this whole week, but I couldn't quite place it. I'm almost beginning to wish my psychic powers would come back. *Almost*." She paused. "Do me a favor..."

"Anything."

"Don't date women like that anymore?"

I laughed. "We were never dating."

She lifted her glass. "Hell of a Valentines Day."

We clinked glasses and sipped the fine whiskey. Hell of a Valentines Day indeed.

46

I sabella called a few days later. "I've got an operative in Mexico that has a visual confirmation on Armando."

That got my attention. "Where?"

"Juan's bar. Armando's prepaid cellular hasn't popped up on the network. I'm sure he's ditched it by now and has another one."

"How long ago?"

"Last night."

"Think he's still in the area?"

"Hard to say. But if you want to find him and bring him back, I wouldn't waste any time."

"Is that an offer of support?"

She paused for a long moment. "I can lend some assets. But you need to do a favor for me."

"Just add it to my tab."

"Your tab is getting quite large, you know that?"

"I know."

Fugitive recovery was the job of the US Marshals. Over the years, they had received varying degrees of assistance from the Mexican government. Mexican law prohibited foreign military and law enforcement agencies from operating within the country, but that didn't mean it never happened. There were long-standing rumors of armed Marshals acting in cooperation with Mexican Marines to recover high-profile fugitives. But I had my doubts that Armando would ever be recovered if we didn't do it ourselves.

I knew what JD's take on the situation would be before I called. He was more than eager to go down there, kick ass, take names, and bring the scumbag back to face justice. If something happened to Armando along the way, so be it.

The last time I was in Mexico, things hadn't gone so well. I had made an unplanned visit to the ER with a gunshot wound. Technically, I died. It was an experience I cared not to revisit. Not until my number was actually up.

Traveling to Mexico with weapons is a dicey proposition. And something best not attempted. More than a few unsuspecting Americans have spent time in a Mexican jail for having a handgun in their glove box when they traveled across the border.

If we decided to proceed with this ill-advised adventure, we'd be solely dependent upon Isabella and her support services. I had no doubt she could provide us with whatever we needed when we were *in country*. But still, if anything went wrong, it wasn't like the Calvary would be coming to save us.

Isabella arranged transportation. A guy named Wyatt Jamison flew us across the Gulf to a little strip of tarmac in Playa that masqueraded as an airport. We swooped over the teal water and white sand beach and touched down on the runway. The tires barked and bounced a little. After several hours in a four-seat prop-engine Cessna, I was ready to find a restroom.

We were both dressed casually—JD wearing his typical Hawaiian shirt and cargo shorts, and me with an *I'd rather be in Mexico* T-shirt. We looked like every other American tourist. I carried a backpack with toiletries, a few days worth of clothes, and plenty of cash—both USD and pesos. Isabella had arranged fake passports, and we breezed through customs.

Wyatt knew the drill. If all went as planned, we would need to leave at a moment's notice once we had acquired the target. I wasn't quite sure how the local officials would take to us escorting a man in handcuffs back to the States, but I figured enough cash in the right palms would cause authorities to look the other way. Keep the wheels greased, and the machine would run smoothly—or so I hoped. I had a little over $20,000 for emergency expenditures. It was probably overkill, but better safe than sorry.

I was traveling under the name Ted Wimberly, and JD's passport identified him as John Dougherty.

We met Isabella's contact at the airport. His name was Dean Anderson. He had short dark hair, a round face, and a slightly round body. He had a light dusting of freckles on his forehead and cheeks, and he looked like your average beer-drinking expat.

"Welcome to Mexico!" he said with a warm smile.

We shook hands, and he escorted us to his car. We climbed in, and he drove us toward our hotel.

"I've got a duffel bag of goodies in the trunk that I think you'll enjoy," Dean said.

"Thank you," I said, looking at his eyes in the rearview mirror. "Much appreciated."

JD sat up front in the passenger seat of the small silver 4-door.

"I saw your target at a local bar not far from here," Dean said. "*Chica Loca*. It's part nightclub, part brothel. It's owned by the cartel and under the control of Juan Valverde. The cartels have their fingers in everything here. If they don't own a place outright, they are extracting a high percentage for *protection*. You need to be careful. There are several warring factions in the area, and at times, it can get quite bloody."

Dean drove us to a luxurious five-star hotel on the beach that was all-inclusive—not that we were here to spend time at the infinity pool, frequenting the swim-up bar, but I didn't know how long our stay would be. Why not stay in style?

Rows of luxury hotels lined the beaches. There were plenty of bikini-clad beauties, swaying palm trees, and blinding tropical sun that glistened toned bodies.

We checked in and made our way to our suite. It had a full kitchen with granite countertops and full-size appliances.

The living space was luxurious with leather furniture, a flatscreen display, and sliding glass doors that opened to a balcony offering a stunning view of the turquoise water and white sand. JD and I each had a private room with an en suite and a queen bed.

"Is this a snatch and grab?" Dean asked, "Or a target elimination?"

47

"**S**natch and grab," I said.

"But we may call an audible on the fly, if necessary," JD added.

Dean unzipped a duffel bag full of goodies. Inside there were several 9mm pistols, extra magazines, flash-bang grenades, and smoke canisters. I snatched a pistol, slapped in a magazine, and pulled the slide, chambering a round. I flipped the weapon on safety, holstered it, then stuffed it in my waistband and covered it with my shirt.

JD did the same.

"I hope everything is to your satisfaction," Dean said.

I smiled. "Yes. Thank you."

"When I saw Armando at *Chica Loca*, he was with a couple of cartel heavy hitters, including Juan Valverde. They were accompanied by a security team of foot soldiers. It's a regular hangout for those guys. Juan is in there almost every night. He likes to fancy himself a singer, so he gets up on the stage with the band and does horrible renditions of American pop and rock songs. I've been keeping tabs on Juan Valverde for some time now. Isabella updated me with your target and asked me to keep an eye out. When I saw Armando, I contacted Isabella immediately."

"What's your interest in Juan Valverde?" I asked.

"I'm not at liberty to discuss that." He paused. "Look, I just gather intel and help with logistics. That's all I do. I leave the shoot 'em up stuff to guys like you."

"I understand," I said. "How long have you been down here?"

"Almost a year. I know this place pretty well. My guess is that Armando is staying at Juan's compound. It's heavily guarded, and I don't recommend any type of takedown there. Plenty of thugs with fully automatic machine guns. Unless you're into that kind of thing."

I exchanged a glance with JD. He shrugged.

"I can show you the compound."

"Sure," I said.

"I gotta tell you, these cartel guys never go anywhere without heavy protection. It's too dangerous. They travel in armored cars. They always have goons with Uzis. It's like a war zone right now. All the cartels are fighting over this patch of turf. You need to pick a very precise window to snatch Armando, and even then, count on it getting messy."

"You don't sound optimistic," I said.

"I'm a realist. And I think you boys should know what you're up against. I mean, how bad do you want this guy? Is it worth it?"

At this point, it was the principle of the thing. I wouldn't be able to sleep easy knowing Armando was walking the streets a free man, enjoying the pleasures of life south of the border. "One way or another, justice will be served."

Dean shrugged as if to say *it's your funeral*. "I'll do whatever I can to help."

We grabbed something to eat at the hotel restaurant. We sat outside, watching the waves crash against the shore. A warm breeze blew throughout the resort. At 84 degrees, it felt downright hot compared to Coconut Key.

After our bellies were full, Dean chauffeured us through town. Juan Valverde lived in an affluent neighborhood. His two-story home had a Spanish tile roof and a large white wall that surrounded the compound. The estate spanned an entire city block. It was a small fortress.

We passed by, and I tried to soak up as much information as I could about the compound. There were two gates facing the main road. One for the garage and one for a pedestrian entrance. Through the slotted iron gate, it was possible to get a glimpse of the courtyard, but not much more than that.

We rounded the block and passed by once again. Dean turned down a side street and drove to the end of the block. He pulled to the curb, and the engine idled. From here, we could see the compound on the corner.

"We can't stay long," Dean said. "Believe me, they've got eyes looking for suspicious cars loitering in the area."

"What about drone surveillance?"

"They've got motion sensors and lookouts. They'll shoot them down if they see them. And they've got local police on the payroll. We might be able to score satellite imagery from Isabella. But I'm telling you... this is not the place to make your move."

We stayed for a few minutes, then Dean dropped the car into gear and pulled away from the curb.

"Your best bet is to hit them at the club and catch them with their pants down," Dean said. "Literally."

We headed across town and drove by Juan's club, surveying the area. Dean gave us an overview of *Chica Loca*, describing the layout, entrances, exits, etc. "Cover charge is a hundred dollars, US."

My brow lifted with surprise. "Sounds a little steep."

"That gets you into the club and free watered-down drinks. It also gives you access to the girls. If you want a little one-on-one time, it's $150 bucks for half an hour. $250 for a full hour. This is a high-class joint. The girls are stunning. They look like something from the pages of a magazine. These aren't streetwalkers that you find for $20 in town. Once you get in this place, you'll understand why these guys go here every night. All the *amenities* are free for them. If I were you, here's what I would do..."

48

Dean shared his plan of attack. It was a good one and in line with what I had in mind.

We had the afternoon and early evening to kill, so we went back to the hotel. Dean said that Juan and Armando probably wouldn't arrive until 9 or 10 PM. They'd drink until they had their fill, then they'd select a companion and disappear into one of the brothel rooms to take care of business.

When the time came, we headed to *Chica Loca* and parked at the curb across the street from the entrance. The garish neon sign cast an array of colors across the street. A sultry silhouette flickered in different poses. The curvaceous neon outline of a nude figure clearly indicated what awaited inside. The exterior was painted in bright yellow, teal, and red. *Chica Loca* gave the appearance of a refined, friendly spot for sex tourism. Despite being owned and operated by the cartel, it was meant to make tourists feel safe and comfortable, like visiting a familiar fast-food restaurant.

Though, the items on the menu were a little more enticing with fewer calories.

We waited outside for an hour until a black SUV pulled to the entrance. Juan and Armando emerged along with two goons. They pushed inside the club, and the SUV sped away to find a parking spot.

We hopped out of the car and jogged across the street. Dean stayed with the vehicle. We'd need a quick getaway.

There was a thick bouncer at the door with slicked-back hair and mustache. We played the role of dumb, drunk tourists. He let us inside and neglected to search us. Drunk gringos were usually considered harmless. The main concern was rival cartels. We paid the cover charge and entered the den of sin.

Music from a live band thumped, playing American pop and rock. At first glance, it looked like your average strip club with colorful lighting, cocktail tables, secluded booths, and a large bar stocked with every imaginable brand of liquor. The shelves behind the bar were illuminated, and colored LEDs under-lit the bar counter. Gorgeous brunettes slinked around chrome poles wearing thigh-high fishnet stockings and garter belts. There was plenty of satin and lace, and the frilly garments contained glorious supple curves.

We hadn't gotten two steps into the club when we were swarmed by a bevy of beauties looking to entice us with their wares. Everything about the place was designed to separate you from your cash. These girls promised to fulfill every fantasy.

We declined their initial offers and made our way to the bar. We ordered a drink, and my eyes scanned the lurid establishment, settling on Juan and Armando. They occupied a booth not far away, and two goons stood guard. Gorgeous girls crowded the booth, pawing on the powerful men. Drinks flowed, and there were smiles and laughs all around.

Juan was a middle-aged guy, bald on top, with short curly hair on the sides. He had a full mustache and wore a white linen suit. He looked every bit the part of a drug overlord. He wore a gaudy gold chain around his neck and several flashy rings. Tufts of chest hair sprouted from his open collar.

The bartender served our drinks, and he eyed JD curiously. After squinting at him for a moment, he said, "I know you."

My heart leapt into my throat. The last thing we needed was to draw attention to ourselves.

The bartender's eyes lit up. "You are the singer, no?"

At first, I was sure the bartender had mistaken JD for the famous '80s rockstar that he resembled. I figured that no one in a joint like this would have heard of *Wild Fury*, though the last video was an Internet sensation and reached #3 on the charts. The video had almost a billion views worldwide.

JD smiled and played it cool.

"I recognize you from the video with the girls," he said, using his hands to illustrate large bosoms. A mischievous grin curled on his face. "*All I need*. Great song!"

I was shocked.

JD had, in fact, been recognized in a foreign country as *Thrash*. It was impressive and somewhat concerning, seeing how we were trying to keep a low profile.

The bartender continued. "The band..." he pointed to the stage, "they play your song every night."

JD lifted an impressed eyebrow and tried not to grin too much.

"You need to get on stage with the band and sing," the bartender said.

JD politely declined.

"You must," the bartender urged enthusiastically.

Then he did something that I had not anticipated. He shouted to Juan Valverde. "Boss! Boss! Come here."

He waved the cartel boss over, but Juan ignored him.

The bartender shouted several more times to get Juan's attention.

Juan dismissed him with a hand wave, but the bartender wouldn't let up.

I was hoping Juan would continue to ignore him. But finally, Juan excused himself from the ladies and strolled to the bartender, looking annoyed. Juan had the confident swagger of a powerful and dangerous man. He was in his own bar, in his element, and he was untouchable.

The excited bartender couldn't contain himself. "Boss, this is him!" he said, pointing at JD. "He's the guy in the video with the gorgeous blondes." He mimicked big bosoms with his hands again. "Your favorite song."

Juan studied JD's face for a moment. Then a wave of recognition washed over him. His eyes lit up. "My friend, I am so honored to have you in my bar!"

The cartel boss extended his hand, and the two shook.

"I am a huge fan," Juan said like a star-struck fan. "Anything you want is on the house. But may I ask one favor?"

Cartel bosses never *asked* for anything. It was a subtle demand.

"You must get up and sing for us." Juan smiled.

It was an offer JD couldn't refuse.

The situation was awkward, to say the least. Fortunately, neither Juan nor Armando had ever seen our faces in the course of the investigation. Neither knew we were cops.

I hoped it would stay that way.

49

Juan wouldn't take no for an answer. And it certainly wasn't wise to make the cartel boss angry. After a round of tequila shots, JD took the stage with Juan, and they both sang *All I Need*.

Juan was quite off-pitch.

But it was his moment to share the stage with an Internet celebrity, so to speak.

Despite Juan's vocal shortcomings, the rendition was met with overwhelming applause. Something told me that every time Juan took the stage, it was met with obligatory enthusiasm.

After the brief set, the boisterous cartel boss invited us back to his table for more drinks. He introduced us to Armando, and I loathed shaking the scumbag's hand.

JD and I played nice.

We indulged in Juan's hospitality, which included seemingly endless shots of tequila and a bevy of willing beauties.

"What brings you to my fair city?" Juan asked.

"A little rest and relaxation," JD said. "Can you ever have too much fun in the sun?"

Juan smiled. "I will make you an honorary lifetime member of the club. No cover charge."

"That's mighty kind of you," JD said.

"We have the finest ladies in all the land, as you can see," Juan said, brimming with pride. The booth was crowded with girls cozying up to all of us.

"These girls will fulfill your heart's desire. But be careful, don't fall in love," Juan cautioned with a maniacal laugh. "But you can fall in lust for an evening."

He lifted his glass to toast, and we swigged the tequila.

"Go ahead and indulge yourself," Juan said. "You pay for nothing here."

JD thanked him for his hospitality.

"That goes for both of you," Juan said, looking at me. "Take your pick. Any girl in the club."

"Except for this one right here," Armando said, pulling a girl named Bonita close.

The girl cooed and whispered something naughty in his ear.

"If you'll excuse me, gentlemen," Armando said. "I think it's time to take care of business. Can't keep the lady waiting."

We slid out of the booth and let Armando exit, dragging his girl in tow.

"I guess it's time for us to take you up on your hospitality," JD said to Juan.

JD escorted a lovely young woman from the booth, and I followed with a companion of my own.

The two girls were used to the routine. They led us through the bar to a staircase, each step lined with red LED strips. Sumptuous hips swayed from side to side as they climbed the steps, their pert cheeks ready to burst through their skimpy, tight skirts. Stiletto heels clacked against the stairs.

When we reached the top of the landing, there was a clerk behind a counter. The girls told him this evening would be compliments of the boss. Normally, this is where you would pay the man for a room. He handed us keys, and the girls guided us down a dimly lit hallway with red walls and black doors. Red LED strips lined the tops of the walls, casting a sinful glow.

There were dozens and dozens of small rooms. Miniature pleasure palaces, rented by the half-hour or hour. Muffled moans and grunts filtered from the rooms. Mattresses squeaked. The girls pulled us down the long corridor, and I made note of which room Armando entered.

We reached our rooms, and Ivette took the key from my hand. She unlocked the door and pulled me inside. The room was small and lit with more red LEDs. I told Ivette to get undressed and wait for me. She smiled and peeled off her dress, then sauntered toward the bed. She looked delicious.

I pulled the door shut and stepped into the hallway. JD had done the same.

There was no one else in the hallway for the time being, and the clerk at the top of the stairs couldn't see from this angle. We waited for a moment. It sounded like someone was coming up the steps. Another girl led a client down the hallway, and we waited for them to enter a room.

When all was clear, we drew our pistols and kicked open the door to Armando's love shack. We barged in, our weapons in the firing position, catching the thug with his pants down. Armando was buck naked on top of the young lady, looking like a dog in heat.

His concubine screeched with terror, and Armando's face twisted with a mix of rage and confusion. He hesitated slightly before reaching for his gun on the nightstand.

"Don't even think about it!" I shouted.

Anger twisted on the thug's face, but he knew he wasn't fast enough to grab his weapon.

"Get off the girl and put your hands against the wall. Now!"

Armando reluctantly complied. "You two are dead men."

"We're all dead men," I replied philosophically. "It's just a matter of time."

JD ratcheted the cuffs around his wrist and twisted his arm behind his back, then brought his other arm around and locked them up tight.

"Make a sound, and I'll blow your ugly head off," JD warned.

"I gotta hand it to you... you guys got balls. Do you have any idea who you're fucking with?"

I poked my head into the hallway and scanned in all directions. Two more girls led clients to rooms. We waited until they disappeared, then we hurried Armando out of his room and down the hallway to a staircase that led to a back exit. The buck-naked thug swayed in the breeze, his bare feet slapping against the tile floor.

JD texted Dean.

When we pushed through the exit door, into the back alley way, Dean was waiting for us. He popped the trunk, and we stuffed Armando inside and slammed the trunk lid. A slew of obscenities flew from Armando's mouth, and he banged and kicked in the trunk.

We hopped into the backseat of the car, and Dean floored it. The tires spit gravel as he peeled out of the alleyway and turned onto a side street.

JD had a shit-eating grin on his face. "Mission accomplished!"

He held out his fist, and we bumped knuckles.

But the celebration was a bit too soon. We weren't out of this yet.

50

The tires squealed as we rounded the corner, and the tiny engine in the four-door sedan howled. Armando kept banging and shouting in the trunk. He was a big guy, and the space was cramped. The ride was probably quite uncomfortable.

I was starting to think we might have gotten away with it when a black SUV fell in line behind us, having pulled out from a side street.

I sat in the backseat, and Dean's nervous eyes flicked to the rearview mirror. "We've got company."

He mashed the pedal to the floor and weaved through the traffic, ignoring street signs. Horns honked, and tires screeched, avoiding narrow collisions.

The SUV rumbled behind us. It's snarling grill inched closer. A pistol emerged from the passenger window.

I rolled down the window and angled my pistol at the behemoth. I squeezed several rounds into the window on the driver's side. Muzzle flash flickered, and bullets peppered the glass, embedding in the windshield. The armored vehicle had bulletproof glass. At best, I'd be able to obstruct the driver's vision.

The SUV probably had run-flat tires, and I was sure there was a protective barrier in the front grill. I pumped a few shots into the engine compartment for good measure, but it didn't seem to do any good. The big, black SUV kept barreling forward.

Dean banked a hard left, and the ass end of the car slid out as we rounded the corner. He counter-steered, keeping it under control, and sped away.

We had one slight advantage over the armored SUV—it was heavy and suffered from massive understeer. When the beast tried to make the corner, it swung wide and plowed into a row of cars parked at the curb. It brushed them away like a tank, scraping paint and showering sparks into the night. It kept going, but the delay opened up a gap between us.

Dean took another hard right, and I tumbled across the back seat and slammed against the opposite door.

I'm sure Armando was enjoying the ride.

Dean banked another hard left and hauled ass down the road, passing storefronts and restaurants.

I looked through the rear window and saw the SUV turn behind us. The V8 thundered, and the SUV gained on us quickly.

Dean swung another left into a residential area, then took a quick right.

We played this cat-and-mouse game, twisting through the streets—and for a moment, I thought we had lost them. We needed to get the hell out of Dodge before the police got involved. They wouldn't be there to help us.

We doubled back around and raced down the boulevard. From the corner of my eye, I saw the massive grill of the SUV launch from a side street. It was on a collision course to T-bone us.

Dean mashed the pedal, and the SUV clipped the right rear quarter panel, sending us into a spiral. Tires shrieked and smoked. Metal crumpled.

The black SUV plowed forward and smacked into a light pole on the opposite corner.

We did a 360 down the roadway, but Dean managed to regain control of the car. He straightened up and kept going, but the right rear tire had been shredded, and the rim ground into the asphalt, spewing sparks as we raced away. He took a hard right, then a left, then another right, and barreled as fast as he could down the road.

I noticed the commotion in the trunk had ceased.

I was pretty sure Armando hadn't survived the impact. The right rear quarter panel had severely encroached upon the narrow compartment.

"Shit," Dean grumbled, his panicked eyes bulging at the instrument cluster on the dash.

"What's the problem?" I asked.

51

"We're running out of gas," Dean shrieked. "Fuel line must have ruptured."

A moment later, flames flickered from the right rear.

Dean pulled into an alley, and we hopped out of the car. The smell of burning gas and rubber filled my nostrils.

We tried to open the trunk, but it was jammed shut from the impact. But let's be honest, we didn't try that hard.

We backed away from the flaming vehicle. It was soon engulfed in an amber glow. It popped and crackled, and black smoke billowed into the night sky. It would be a beacon for the cartel.

Armando would soon be extra crispy.

We took off running down the alley and made a couple of twists and turns through a residential neighborhood.

Dogs barked.

We were far from the tourist part of town. Three gringos wandering these streets would stick out like sore thumbs.

We found an abandoned home a few blocks away. There was no roof, and the exposed cinder block was damaged and crumbling in parts. The derelict structure was overgrown with weeds and was loosely fenced off with chicken wire. Two main walls had fallen down. There was a pile of gravel and some construction materials in the area. Who knows how long it had been standing there?

There was another vacant lot next to it and beside that a lime-green home that was still occupied. Across the street was a brand new 6-unit, two-story apartment building.

We took cover in the desolate structure and hid there for quite a while.

The stars flickered overhead, and crickets chirped.

The black SUV cruised through the neighborhood, searching for us. We crouched low as it rolled by the abandoned structure, a flashlight beam slashing the night.

We waited until the vehicle turned the corner.

There was a red Jeep parked at the curb with the windows and top down. When all was clear, Dean left the shelter of the building, ran down the sidewalk, and slinked inside the Jeep. Within a few minutes, he had the vehicle started. We dashed to the Jeep and hopped inside. Dean drove casually out of the neighborhood.

I called Wyatt and told him we were ready for an immediate evacuation. Dean drove us straight to the airport, and we ditched the Jeep and the guns. We shook hands and thanked him for his assistance, just as the sun crested the horizon. Dean hopped into a cab, and I never saw him again.

I was starting to breathe easier, but we weren't out of this yet.

We were walking across the tarmac to Wyatt's Cessna when we were suddenly surrounded by Mexican Police. There was no doubt that the cartel had put the word out to law enforcement to look for three Americans on the run. Angry barrels of fully automatic assault rifles stared at us. We were only a few yards away from the aircraft—a few steps to freedom.

My stomach twisted, and I envisioned a lifetime in a crappy cell with no running water and only a slop bucket. Maybe a crusty slice of bread and a gulp of nasty water per day, if I was lucky. Then I realized I didn't have to worry about a lifetime in a Mexican prison. We'd be handed over to the cartel and dealt with accordingly.

We raised our hands in the air and exchanged wary glances.

52

I told the police in Spanish, "In my backpack, you'll find an exit fee. We must have forgotten to pay it." I smiled. "My apologies."

An officer approached and took my backpack. He looked inside and found my clothes and the two fat stacks of $100 bills. About $20,000, plus several thousand pesos. The officer held up the loot. The other policemen surveyed the cash and exchanged glances.

It was hard to say how this would go down. They'd either take the money and let us go or take the money and hand us to the cartel.

There was a long, uncomfortable silence.

The sergeant finally nodded to his crew, and their weapons lowered. In English, he said, "Enjoy your flight, gentlemen."

With that, the squad dispersed, and we proceeded to the aircraft. We climbed aboard, and Wyatt went through the preflight checks. It was a long nervous few minutes as we waited to be cleared for takeoff. Finally, we raced down the runway. The nose lifted off the ground, and soon we were angling towards the sky, flying over the teal water.

I breathed a sigh of relief and leaned back in my seat.

Mission accomplished. Sort of.

When we got back to Coconut Key, I was ready for a good meal, a stiff drink, and a little relaxation. I called Shiloh and told her she didn't have to worry about Armando anymore. But I couldn't say that she would be safe from Juan Valverde or the cartel. For that matter, I couldn't say that we were safe from Juan Valverde or the cartel.

Shiloh decided to enter the Witness Security Program, and I wished her well in her new life.

I had slept on the flight back home, recharging my batteries slightly. After a shower and a change of clothes, I was ready for a nice dinner. JD joined me at *Diver Down,* and we feasted like kings. Teagan worked the bar and seemed like she was getting along okay after the traumatic incident.

"I'm not even going to ask what happened down there," she said.

"It's better if you don't," I replied with a grin. "Although JD is now officially an international celebrity."

Teagan's brow knitted, not quite sure what to make of my comment.

My phone buzzed with a call from Chloe-C. Her album was topping the charts, and her world tour was selling out every venue. She'd call me sporadically between gigs. Her voice was a little raspy from singing every night. "I can't talk long.

I just wanted to let you know, due to scheduling conflicts, we've got two dates in NY without an opening act. *Wild Fury* can have them, but I need to know by tomorrow. I'm talking two nights in the Garden... sold out."

Since I was now the manager of the band, I said, "I'll run it by JD and see what he says."

I couldn't imagine the band turning down the opportunity. I thanked Chloe and told her I'd be in touch.

Daniels called shortly thereafter. I caught him up to speed on our little excursion. "Well, rest up. You know what's coming next."

The spring was always a chaotic season in Coconut Key. It was a nonstop month of mayhem. Throngs of college students from all across the country descended upon the island every year to drink, raise hell, and hook up with random strangers.

The influx of teeny bikinis came with a downside— increased traffic, drunk and disorderly crowds, and emergency rooms packed with college kids that had overindulged. Last year, we dealt with a particularly heinous predator. I was optimistic that this spring break would be relatively tame.

But I was wrong.

Ready for more?

The adventure continues with Wild Spring!

Join my newsletter and find out what happens next!

AUTHOR'S NOTE

Thanks for all the great reviews!

I've got more adventures for Tyson and JD. Stay tuned.

If you liked this book, let me know with a review on Amazon.

Hope you are well during this challenging time. Thanks for reading!

—*Tripp*

TYSON WILD

Wild Ocean

Wild Justice

Wild Rivera

Wild Tide

Wild Rain

Wild Captive

Wild Killer

Wild Honor

Wild Gold

Wild Case

Wild Crown

Wild Break

Wild Fury

Wild Surge

Wild Impact

Wild L.A.

Wild High

Wild Abyss

Wild Life

Wild Spirit

Wild Thunder

Wild Season

Wild Rage

Wild Heart

Wild Spring

Wild Outlaw

Wild...

CONNECT WITH ME

I'm just a geek who loves to write. Follow me on Facebook.

www.trippellis.com

Made in United States
North Haven, CT
15 April 2023

35456414R10171